Jane Gay Fuller

The Brownings

A Tale of the Great Rebellion

Jane Gay Fuller

The Brownings
A Tale of the Great Rebellion

ISBN/EAN: 9783337023416

Printed in Europe, USA, Canada, Australia, Japan

Cover: Foto ©Andreas Hilbeck / pixelio.de

More available books at **www.hansebooks.com**

THE BROWNINGS.

THE ATTACK ON ROSE COTTAGE.

THE BROWNINGS.

A TALE OF THE

GREAT REBELLION

NEW YORK:

M. W. DODD, No. 506 BROADWAY.

A TALE OF THE

GREAT REBELLION.

BY

J. G. FULLER,

AUTHOR OF "THE GRAHAMS," ETC.

———

NEW YORK:

M. W. DODD, 506 BROADWAY,

1867.

THE NEW YORK PRINTING COMPANY,
81, 83, and 85 Centre Street,
NEW YORK.

THE BROWNINGS.

CHAPTER I.

I WISH you a "merry Christmas," and will tell you a story.

You must not think, my young readers, that it is cold everywhere at Christmas, and that children are obliged to go out muffled and fur-red as they do here. In our own country there are many places where the sun shines warmly, and the flowers blossom all the year round. While the happy children of the North have merry sleigh-rides and go skating on the frozen ponds and rivers, the little ones of the sunny South pick oranges and pomegranates, or twine garlands of roses for the "merry Christmas" days.

If you have studied geography, you will recollect that the St. Mary's river forms a part of the boundary line between the States of Georgia and Florida. On the banks of this river, only a few miles from its entrance into the Atlantic Ocean, there stood not long ago a pretty rustic cottage, covered all over with scarlet woodbine and white Cherokee roses. It was not a solid, substantial-looking building, such as you see everywhere at the North, built for protection against frost and storm; it looked more like a summer-house or arbor built for ornament rather than use. It *was* a summer-house, and its doors and windows were seldom closed; for although the children of the St. Mary's count December, January, and February in the months of the year, they seldom see there either frost or snow.

On Christmas morning, 1861, a little white girl dressed in black, and a large black girl dressed in white, were sitting together on the piazza of the cottage. They had a basket of flowers before them, and the large one was try- ing her skill at making a wreath. The little **girl's name was** Lucy Browning, but her friends all called her Lulu. The colored girl **was** her nurse—Teenah. Teenah looked **as** black as ebony in her white dress, while little Lulu in her black one looked pale as a snowdrop.

It had **not been** a "merry Christmas" morn- ing at the cottage, for many reasons. Lulu comprehended but one. Since the last Christ- mas her beautiful mother had gone away from them to dwell with the angels. She did not quite comprehend that, even; only that her mother was gone from **the** cottage and was laid under the green oaks at the **end** of the lawn, where little Lulu **went** every even- ing to say "Our Father," and sing the even- ing hymn her mother taught **her.** Only the Christmas before, she had sung her **a** sweet little carol and tied her a garland of rose-buds; and when her father went out that morning with his dog and gun, he raised her in his arms, pressed her to his heart, and said : " Go, Lula, and sing to darling mamma to-day! Sing the Christ-child and carry roses." Then he kissed her and pressed her to his heart again.

Lulu followed him to the river bank, watched him while he untied the little skiff at the landing, saw him jump in with old Zack the hunter, then threw kisses after him all the way across the river to Florida.

"There, he has got there now, Teenah! Don't you see? Make haste, and let us go and cut sweet roses for mamma."

While Lulu and her nurse are in the garden, we will look around and see what we can discover.

Groups of oleanders taller than the cottage are all in bloom **on** one side ; on the other is an orangery, every tree hanging with ripe fruit and budding with snowy flowers. Behind the house is a little cluster of cabins ; before one of these, an old grey-haired negro sits in the sun playing the violin : but there are no dancers, as usual on Christmas morning.

The cabins are deserted. If you watch the old man closely you will see him now and then take a corner of his bright bandanna and wipe his eyes. He is weeping, not for himself, but for his dear young master. One of the strings of his instrument snapped at last under his heavy stroke. " 'Pears like 'tis another of poor Mar's Alfred's heartstrings," he said softly ; " hunted like a wild beast by the wicked Seceshers. Nothin' for ole Dick any more but to watch and wait!" and his tears grew to sobs.

An old woman with a pipe in her mouth and a gay head-dress came out of the cabin.

"Dis yer won't do nohow, ole man," she said almost sternly. "It neber 'll do! Don't you see how I bears up? Go to the patch ober dar, now, and bring some yams and some cabbage and turnips; de Christmas-turkey is on the spit, and Miss Lulu's pie is baking full of plums. I tell you, ole man, 'twon't do fur to be idle. No more holidays for de like ob us till we git de long freedom. When Mar's

Alfred said de udder day, ' Aunt Chrissy, you can go if you like; de way is open now,' I tole him we is ole people, you and I, and will wait for de hebenly gates to open. But 'tis time you is up and gwine now, ole man! We will hab de dinner all ready when young Massa comes."

Uncle Dick got up slowly and walked away in the direction of the field. In the garden he met little Lulu and Teenah returning to the cottage with their flowers, and waited to give them a Christmas blessing.

Only two short years before, and Rose Cottage was one of the happiest homes in the South; I did not say the *wealthiest*, for in the rich Gulf States there were many *richer* men than Alfred Browning, Lulu's father. Only a little further down the river was a planter thrice as rich as he, and it was at this same planter's he made the acquaintance of the fair stranger who afterwards became his wife. It proved a happy union for both, though existing but five years.

Little Lulu's mother was a native of New Hampshire. Her father had died of consumption before she was fifteen. She had one brother older than herself in college at the time of her father's death. Her mother was left in moderate circumstances; but understanding her husband's wishes in regard to the education of her children, she determined to execute them faithfully. John was sent back to college, and Ellen to a neighboring seminary, while their mother toiled early and late for their support. In spite of her best efforts, however, debts accumulated, and the pretty homestead was mortgaged for half its value.

"It will be better by and by," the mother said hopefully. "John will have his profession, and Ellen can teach school; then I shall lay up something, instead of falling back. It is of no use to trouble them about it now."

It was their last year at school, and the widow calculated rightly in regard to future expenses; but wrongly when estimating her

daughter's strength to endure the wear and
tear of a teacher's life. The first quarter's
trial was robbing her cheeks of their bloom
and developing the seeds of latent disease,
when an accident changed the sphere of her
labors.

One summer afternoon, the village innkeep-
er called upon Mrs. Hunter to ask a favor for
a stranger. A lady on her way to the mountains had met with an accident which might
detain her for several days in the village. His
house was crowded and noisy; the lady needed
quiet and repose. Would she entertain her
and her daughter until the arrival of her husband from Washington?

Mrs. Hunter had no objection to offer, and
the same evening found the strangers comfortably located in her pleasant home. A warm
attachment was the result; and before the arrival of her husband, Mrs. McIntosh was
urging Mrs. Hunter to allow her **daughter**
to return with them to Georgia in the autumn.

"We cannot afford it," the mother replied, with simple frankness. "I have no doubt the change might benefit her as you say, and I would gladly yield my own wishes for her good; but at present it is not to be thought of."

"We will defray all her expenses," the lady persisted.

"I could not accept your invitation on those terms," interposed Ellen. "Independence is more necessary to me than either health or pleasure."

"Why wouldn't Miss Ellen go and be our teacher?" Ally McIntosh asked, on another occasion. "It wouldn't be so hard for her as her school here, and we want her so much."

No one replied; but when Mr. McIntosh came, the subject was resumed. In speaking of her school one day, he inquired the number of her pupils and her salary.

"Twenty-five pupils, and thirty dollars a month," was the reply.

"I will give you **fifty** dollars a month for

three pupils," he returned. "My wife and
Ally will not be persuaded to go home without you. Think of it until our return from
the Notch, and then give us your decision."

"I will give it now, sir," she said, pleasantly.
"If my mother consents, I should be very
happy to accept your offer."

Mrs. Hunter offered no objection, and two
months later Ellen Hunter accompanied her
new friends South. That was the way Lulu's
mother first went to the St. Mary's. Alfred
Browning was a nephew of the gentleman, and
found his uncle's house more agreeable than
ever after the advent of the Northern teacher,
who was treated in every respect like a daughter of the house.

Two years afterwards, Ellen went back to
New Hampshire with a sum of money sufficient to pay up what remained of the old mort-
gage, her mother and brother having already
reduced it to a third of its original amount;
and that same autumn, a gay Southern party

came to take her again to Georgia—not to McIntosh Grove, but to Rose Cottage, her future home.

CHAPTER II.

THERE are some natures that seem formed to awaken love wherever they go. Ellen Browning's was such a one. Far away amid the hills where her happy childhood was passed, she was the pet and pride of her native village. On the banks of the St. Mary's, surrounded with strangers, strange customs and institutions, she was soon beloved by the lofty and lowly who shared her acquaintance; and never was bride more warmly welcomed than she was to Rose Cottage plantation. Men who made it a point to dislike New England, and delighted to express their sentiments on every occasion, forgot their prejudices in the presence of Ellen Browning, and congratulated her husband on the worth of his prize.

No home in all the region was so well regu-

lated as theirs. Not a dusky finger-mark remained on its walls. All the freshness and
neatness of a Northern home seemed united to
the bloom and sunshine of the South. The
bride's own hands looped back the snowy
muslin and disposed the simple furniture of
her apartments, hung the pictures on the walls,
grouped the flowers in the vases, and the most
fastidious could detect no want of harmony.
Visitors surprised her at her morning tasks,
and she received them without apology, just as
she sang and played to them without affecta-
tion or vanity.

Of all her dusky house-maids, not one could
catch the secret of their young mistress's ways
except the child Teenah, whose instinctive love
of beauty and order seemed the very counter-
part of her own. She was a little thing,
scarcely eight years old, and clung to **Mrs.**
Browning like her shadow. It was not long
before she surprised her with bouquets of fault-
less structure, and often in the morning her
self-imposed tasks were anticipated and per-

formed with the most scrupulous neatness and exactness by the careful child. Teenah soon became the favored attendant of her mistress; sat at her feet and learned to sew, and sing, and read, until the advent of little Lulu divided her care.

"May I *love* the baby, Miss Ellen?" was the singular inquiry of the little black nurse, as she sat a few days after, waving her great fan over the infant's crib.

"What do you mean, Teenah?"

"Do no what I mean, Missus! Never had noffin to love much! No mammy, no baby!"

"Do you remember your mother, Teenah?"

"Never had none, only Aunt Chrissy."

"Who taught you before I came?"

"De birds, Miss!"

The eyes of the young mother filled with tears. A little human heart crying out from its lonely depths for love, for something to love, was a thing she had never thought of before. There were a dozen children on the plantation; how it happened that Teenah had

no brother or sister among them, no home in
their cabins, she could not tell. " Will MY
child ever know such poverty of heart?" she
thought, as she gazed on the solitary waif
before her; "God alone knows."

After a silent prayer for direction, Ellen
Browning called her little maid to her side.

"I have not answered your question yet,
Teenah. Will you love my baby?"

" Better than anything in de world, if you
will let me, Miss."

"Love her all you wish, my poor child.
Teach her the things I have taught you, and
other things I will teach you, when she has no
mother."

"Out of de pictur' book, Miss?"

"Out of another book, Teenah. I will teach
you about God and heaven."

"Oh, I know *Him* now, Miss Ellen. He
MADE me. Did He make all de darkeys?"

" Yes, and the white folks too."

" Why didn't He make dem like, den?"

A hearty laugh outside betrayed a listener.

"Good for YOU, little ebony," said the voice of Alfred Browning. "I will send you to *Oberlin* when Miss Ellen has exhausted her stock of knowledge, especially if you are to be the future teacher of Lulu."

There was something ironic in the tone of her husband's voice; but the hearty laugh that succeeded was full of good-nature, and reassured her.

"Come in, Alfréd, and sit by the crib while Teenah cuts me some flowers."

There was a merry smile lurking in the corner of his mouth as he obeyed the summons.

"Shall I use the brush *this* way?" he asked, demurely. "Now, Ellen, what is it?"

"Tell me who is Teenah, and why she has no relatives on the plantation?"

"A little shipwrecked imp, I bought for a few shillings off the coast, and brought home to Aunt Chriss."

"How did it all happen?"

"Half-a-dozen years ago a terrible storm occurred. Many vessels were wrecked off the

Carolinas, and among them an African slaver. Her captain **was** from Cape Cod, and his worthless carcass became food for sharks. Many dead bodies were washed ashore, and among them an old colored sailor who had Teenah lashed to his back. The child was alive, and in a few hours was as active as a monkey. I was up the coast not long after, and heard that a few of the surviving negroes were at the house of a wrecker. Being short of hands at the time, I went to look at them; but a Florida trader was there before me. He had taken them all with the exception of the child, whom the wrecker's wife was most anxious to be rid of. I took her, out of sheer pity to both, and she bids fair to become a genius."

"I will see what I can make of her," returned his wife, gravely. "You know I have always liked the child."

And so for nearly four years Teenah grew under the kindly fostering care of the new mistress, a highly favored child of bondage. And

3

when her mistress's strength declined, all the care that had been bestowed upon her was repaid a hundredfold by the grateful child. Of all the attached servants no one knew as well as she how to minister to the invalid's pleasure or her necessities. No one else could sing her own cradle-song to little Lulu, and to no one save her parents was the little one so fondly attached. Even Alfred Browning had to acknowledge at last that "Teenah was no common darkey."

Very difficult it is when skies are bright, and the voice of love whispers of a happy future, to respond, "Our future lies not here! It is hidden in the grave!" Ellen Browning found it so, and so for awhile kept silent. But when the war-clouds began to gather in her country's horizon, and she heard the distant angry thunder and felt assured the tempest would not pass by, her own life appeared to her of little moment in comparison with a duty left undone, or a word of truth left unspoken. Then for the first time since she had forsaken her own home for that of strangers was the voice of **de**-traction raised against her.

With few exceptions, **the** landed proprietors **of that** vicinity favored the new political party. **Her old** friends, the McIntoshes, **were** among the leaders. As a near relative **of** the family, her husband's decision rested with great weight upon her mind. A convention had been called **at** the capital for State action. The question whether he would **assist** to swell the tide of disloyalty was more to **her** then than whether she would **live to** bless his life or watch **over** their child.

Never from woman's lips have arisen more earnest cries than from hers that her husband's feet might not stumble on the dark mountain of secession; never from woman's **eyes** fallen more joyful **tears** than from hers when she heard him respond **to a** party **of** friends, who came to question him openly—" **I am** not with you in this matter. Every **drop of** blood **in** my veins is loyal **to** the old Union!"

Not a word on **the** subject had ever passed

between them; but when their guests were gone, she drew her chair close beside him, took his hand and pressed it to her lips, saying:

"I can bear to die now, my husband! You have lifted the heaviest weight from **my** heart."

"*Bear to die*, Ellen! Tell me what you mean, darling?"

"Don't look so shocked! Gaze calmly upon me, Alfred, and now you will see how very near I am drawing to our Eternal Home. I could not bear to speak of it; I thought you **would see it soon** enough. But joy has unsealed my lips. While I have prayed once that you might be able to bear this stroke without complaint, I have prayed many times that you might be strong in the hour of our country's darkness. God be thanked that you are true and loyal!"

"This subject has tried you too far, my dear, and you have grown weak and nervous. Do **not** think I have been blind to your anxiety, or that it has not influenced me. Although

my own convictions would for ever have prevented me from being a secessionist, I might
have been tempted, like **many** others, **to** drift
along **with the** popular **current,** instead **of** re-
solving steadily to oppose it. Do not think
that the loss of property or a sense of personal
danger could have influenced me; but issues
dearer far than my own life are involved in
my decision—the safety perhaps of my wife
and child."

" Fear not for us, Alfred ; I shall soon be at
rest, and the God who has heard my prayers
will watch over our child."

" I cannot bear to hear you speak thus, my
darling wife; you unnerve me. When the
winter passes away from your Northern hills,
I will send you to gather strength in their
bracing air. Have courage until then, Ellen ! "

She smiled faintly. Her husband turned
and brushed away a tear.

CHAPTER III.

No sooner were Alfred Browning's political sentiments avowed than the tide of public opinion turned against him; and by none was he more strongly reproached than by his own kindred. "They had always suspected him of leaning towards abolitionism," they averred; "his marriage to a Northerner had doubtless strengthened that inclination. But one thing was certain; he could never live in peace, and share the benefits of a government he ignored. Georgia was an independent State, for ever cut loose from the old Union; and her sons must abide the decision or become outcasts."

The taunt of abolitionism stirred the proud spirit of Browning to its very depth, while the allusion to his marriage stung him to anger.

"If," he said haughtily, "to hold a State institution lightly, when it conflicts with the welfare of my country, constitute an abolitionist, then am I one indeed, though I never before had such a suspicion. And if to have married a woman of goodness above all praise strengthen not a man's courage *to do right*, he must be altogether unworthy of his good fortune."

As time sped, that which had long been apparent to the young wife and mother became evident to all. The spoiler was not to be robbed of his prey by soft sunshine, change of air, or the sweeter breath of love. His claim had already been delayed a few pleasant years, while earth-ties had been growing stronger and stronger. Had she remained in her own Northern home, the seeds of disease would doubtless have matured a little sooner, but not more certainly; for when were the seeds of consumption, once planted, ever known to fail?

The certainty of the event fell with crushing weight upon the faithful husband, who had shut his eyes steadily against conviction. For awhile he could not be brought to speak on the subject, or act in reference to it. But in time a portion of his wife's heroic spirit seemed infused into his own, though little of her patient submission. Her wishes in regard to the future of her child were in strict accordance with his own. She had another wish, more earnestly expressed even than those for her own child, and lived to see it gratified. It was Teenah's emancipation. The legal papers were drawn and placed in her own hands, and she had the satisfaction of communicating the intelligence to the child, and advising her as to her future.

Lulu's nurse wept on her knees as the information was imparted to her; kissed her kind mistress's hands, and promised never to leave her little helpless charge to a stranger, whatever might happen. The promise was a comfort to the dying parent.

The other servants of the estate shared their young mistress's care and blessing; and when her last work of love was done, and they laid her to rest beneath the flowers of June, all the sunshine of Rose Cottage was darkened for ever.

Great events in the history of the nation trod thickly upon one another in the succeeding months. The war-cloud which lay dark and threatening in the horizon burst in fury on the land. The victory of Manassas had inspired the Southern leaders with fresh confidence and determination, and no voice of reason was thenceforward heard in cabinet or council. Every man, whatever his wishes or his will, must **help to** drive the car of their Moloch through the land. **No** Union man was safe to abide in peace at home.

Several times since refusing to enrol his name **as** a volunteer in the rebel service Alfred Browning had been warned to repair to a camp of instruction, or prepare for a worse fate. Threats did not intimidate him. "*Truth must have its martyrs,*" he said haughtily. "If I die, it shall be in its defence." He had asked but one boon—to send his little one and her nurse to her mother's friends in the North,

5

"*No one will be permitted to leave the Confederacy*," was the tyrannous reply.

It was not long before the granary of the plantation was rifled of its corn, and the sugarhouse of its sweets. His flocks were also driven away by the merciless guerillas.

"It is the last food Rose Cottage plantation will ever furnish the rebellion," he said resolutely.

A few days afterwards he called together his field-hands and addressed them thus:

"We have been robbed of our crops by the guerillas. If there is anything to entice them, we shall be robbed again. I will plant no more. You have heard of the great fleet that has landed upon the islands of the coast. The Northerners come to liberate the white men of the South as well as the blacks. I will do all in my power to assist them. As many of you as are willing to take your lives in your hands and run your chances of getting to the fleet are at liberty to go. You have all been faithful to me, but I have no further need

of your services. You are now *free*. I promised your dying mistress to care for you, and
will do my best to provide you with extra
clothing for the coming year. Take what
provisions you may require for the journey,
and help one another. The way is not long;
go a few at a time; and if you are arrested
and brought back as runaways, you can start
again. I will do all I can for you, and may
God guide you in safety!"

A shower of tears and sobs burst from the
poor creatures while their master was speaking.

"God bress dear Mar's Alfred," was heard on
every side. But only a few appeared in haste
to avail themselves of the proffered freedom;
for the plantation, especially since the advent
of the beloved mistress, had been a home of
comfort to them as well as of toil.

There is much error in the common belief
that *cruelty* is the law of the Southern plantation. It is only an exception to the more
general rule of care and kindness. Wrong as

such a system of servitude may be in itself, great as are its attendant evils, nowhere perhaps in the world **are** found more careless, happy laborers than in the Southern United States.

In **less than a** month every cabin on the estate, except old Uncle Dick's, was deserted. They went in families and companies, **and** their exodus was attended with **much** unfeigned sorrow. Some **of** them **were** old servants— the playmates of their master in his boyhood ; and a few older still, brought by the *old* master **when he** came out from South Carolina thirty years before. These needed a word of encouragement as they went forth like helpless **children** to an untried life.

Aunt Chrissy alone was incorrigible.

"Let the chilluns **go out** mid **songs and** thanksgivin's," she said. "Uncle Dick and I is ole people, and will wait for dem on de *shinin' shore.* Young Mar's was rocked in dis yer ole arms, and dey'll work for him till dar work **is** done."

Uncle Dick abided by Aunt Chrissy's decision, while their children and grandchildren went forth **to** freedom; **and** this **is why the** cabins **were all** deserted **on** Christmas morning.

CHAPTER IV.

WE will now go back to little Lulu and
Teenah, whom we left making wreaths on the
piazza.

When they had completed them, they went
away through the orangery to lay their offer-
ings on the new-made grave. It was a lovely
spot. Purple passion-flowers and yellow jas-
mines ran wild on every side. They crept up
the tall oaks, hid in the pendulous mass, and
sent their perfume down like a breath of love
to the little motherless child, who threw herself on the green sod, and wept as though her
heart were breaking. Teenah wept, too, as she
strove to comfort her. She told her her mamma
wasn't sick any more, like she was before;
that the good angels had carried her away to
their own beautiful country, and put a gold

crown on her head, and a harp in her hand ; and that when she had learned all the pretty **stories** there, and all the **sweet** hymns, she would come back for Lulu.

" And papa ? " asked the child.

" Yes, for Mar's Alfred too ; and maybe de good Lord will send for Teenah."

"Oh ! I shall take *you* when I go, Teenah,". said **Lulu,** very gravely. " You know I couldn't get along without you ; I couldn't curl my hair, or make wreaths, or do anything ; and mamma will wish to see you when I come, you know. Mamma loved you, Teenah."

Then the little ones began to sing, and sang all the Christmas hymns they knew, while the sun crept up the heavens until noon.

Not long after, Uncle Dick might have been seen walking slowly through the shrubbery towards the oak grove. He had his old fiddle under his arm, and some cakes in his hands which Aunt Chrissy had sent for the children.

Lulu had sung herself to sleep, and lay with her head in Teenah's lap. Uncle Dick ob-

served this, and not wishing to disturb her,
sat down at a respectful distance and began to
pull the strings of his beloved instrument in a
way that made it respond very sadly. By and
by he bowed his head as though keeping time
to some remembered tune, then broke out in
mournful tenor:

> " Dar'll be no more sorrow dar—
> Dar'll be no more sorrow dar !
> In heben above, whar all is love,
> Dar'll be no more sorrow dar ! "

The sound of his voice aroused the little
sleeper. She looked around and whispered:
"I thought the angels were coming for us,
Teenah ; but it is only Uncle Dick."

Seeing a shade of disappointment on Lulu's
face, Teenah said, laughingly: " He's got plum-
cakes to do us till dinner. Look yer! Now,
Uncle Dick, play us a real lively tune; den
we'll go and watch for Mar's Alfred."

An hour afterwards the children were sitting upon the wharf, but neither boat nor

boatmen could be seen. The Christmas dinner was ready and waiting, and Uncle Dick
was walking backwards and forwards between
the kitchen and the landing-place until the
report of a gun was heard in an opposite direction.

"Didn't tink Massur 'd come that way," he
said; and went to **see what** he could discover.

He was scarcely out of sight, when two men
with blue cockades on their hats made their
appearance on the wharf.

"Good morning, Cousin Fred," said Lulu.

"A merry Christmas, little fairy! What
are you looking for here at the landing?"

"For the boat, with papa and old Zack."

"Oh, he went this way, then," said the gentleman in a significant tone to his companion.
"How long since he went away, little cousin?"

Aunt Chrissy came hurrying down to the
wharf, shaking her head at the children, and
asking a dozen questions of the men before
they had time to reply to the first.

"Had they heard a word about de runaway darkeys? Poor Mar's Alfred was done worn out hunting for dem. Not a soul left to clar de field, and all de corn and sugar clean gone with them. Any ob ole Mar's Tom's darkeys run away to de ole Union?"

In the midst of her questioning they beat a hasty retreat.

"Chile," said Aunt Chrissy, addressing Lulu when the men were out of sight, "you oughtn't to have tole dem dar men what you's looking for."

"Mamma taught me to speak the truth," Lulu replied, solemnly.

"Truth is pearls! Bad men is swine. 'Twon't do nohow for to cast de pearls afore de swine. My good ole Missus use for to say dat ar to me."

Lulu understood nothing of all this. She only felt as though she had done wrong in some way, and could hardly keep from crying, especially when another hour passed and her father did not come.

If the hours of that afternoon were long, the winter days were very short; and the sun soon began to sink in the west, and the long shadows to fall eastward. Aunt Chrissy called Lulu and Teenah to the kitchen to eat their Christmas pies, and said they would have dinner by lamplight.

But long after lamplight no one had tasted dinner at Rose Cottage. The turkey was cold on the table; all the nice vegetables which had been moulded in pretty forms were cold also: only the coffee was boiling and fragrant on the kitchen hearth. The night was dark and hazy; and Uncle Dick with his lantern sat upon the lonely wharf waiting for his master until midnight, then went back to the kitchen to communicate his fears to Aunt Chrissy.

Lulu was asleep in her arms; she could not put her to bed, she said, before Mar's Alfred came. Teenah lay upon the floor with her back to the fire thinking of the old Christmas times when mirth and gladness ruled the festival until its close, and the beloved Mistress was both gift-giver and angel.

CHAPTER V.

NOT long after midnight, the sound of cautious footsteps was heard in the path that led from the cottage to the kitchen; then the latch-spring was drawn and the door opened.

"Bress God! Mar's Alfred, you is safe," exclaimed Aunt Chrissy.

Every one else in the cabin was asleep apparently, and no one was awakened by his noiseless entrance. The fire had burned down to a few brands, but before it stood the coffeepot; and the old woman made a movement as if to rise and wait upon him.

"Keep quiet, and let me speak to you. The guerillas are on my track again, and threaten to make clean work. My uncle's man, Tim, has revealed the whole plot. I wish to speak of the children, and no time is to be lost. You must take them away to-night. Take them to the old cabin on Little Creek, and remain there until you see or hear from me. Uncle Dick can supply you with fish and wild game, and Tim will carry you hominy and rice. Here is a small trunk which contains gold and my mother's jewels. Preserve it, if possible, for Lulu. There are valuable papers in the trunk also."

Teenah was no longer asleep. Her large, dark eyes were fixed intently upon her master, while her ears drank in every word he had spoken.

"Trust it wid me," she said, earnestly, as she arose and stood before him. "I will save it for Miss Lulu."

"I have to trust *her* to your care, Teenah. Whatever happen, promise me you will never forsake her."

"I would die first, Mar's Alfred. I know all de paths in de woods to Little Creek; and my eyes are not old, nor my ears deaf, like Uncle Dick's. You may trust Lulu to me."

Aunt Chrissy put the child gently in her father's arms, then aroused Dick, and went away to the cottage where the Christmas dinner had been waiting for long hours on the table. Lulu's little bed was tied in a close bundle, and a few garments from her wardrobe were added to it. A large basket was next filled with food from the table and a few culinary utensils; then warm shawls were found, and Lulu was wrapped closely without awaking.

"What will *you* do, Mar's Alfred?" Teenah asked sadly, as they were making ready to depart.

"Stay and defend the house at all hazards."

"Dey'll tar you to pieces like tiger-cats," said Uncle Dick, groaning aloud.

"I have to die some time, Dick, and dare them to do their worst."

"Dar's de chile, den?"

"Yes, the child. My poor little Lulu!" he exclaimed, pressing her to his heart, while tears rolled down his cheeks. "Better that you were laid beside your angel mother, **my bird of paradise!** Are you all ready? Come, then, I will carry her a little way and be back in time."

All through the **pine** regions **of** the far South may be found little hovels without occupants. They belong **to the** cow-hunters. Many of the wealthy planters have immense herds of cattle. In the autumn these cattle are all driven forth to distant fields to subsist during the winter months. When spring arrives, **a** party of men **on** horseback, with long whips **and** trained dogs, go forth to **hunt the cows and** bring them home with their young calves to **the** plantation-pens. Sometimes they stray away many miles, **and the** hunters are **out** for days scouring the **wood**-paths and **green savannas** before they discover their own mark ; for every drove has **its** owner's mark. Saddle-bags of provision **and** blankets are taken by the hunters, and these lonely lodges are their shelter from night and storm. They are commonly **located near some**

creek or spring of water, and sometimes an
old camp-kettle or tea-kettle will be found
secreted within. Runaways are often surprised and captured in these desolate cabins,
but never in the season of cow-hunting.

Towards one of those wretched cabins were
the footsteps of our fugitives now directed. It
was nearly five miles from the cottage, on the
bank of a little creek bordered on one side by
a green prairie meadow, on the other by thick
pine woods. The cabin stood in the woods.
Two years before the family went there for a
day's fishing, and had a merry time of it.
Both Teenah and Aunt Chrissy were of the
party, and Teenah had not forgotten it. Often
in imagination had she wandered back to that
solitary cabin; and when, at the distance of a
mile or so from the cottage, her master inquired
if they were certain of the paths, Teenah described every crook and turn of the way to his
entire satisfaction. Aunt Chrissy had never a
sharp eye for locality or direction, and Uncle
Dick was long past being trusted for anything

7

except correct intentions. Though he had been a hundred times to the spot, he would very likely have missed it in the dimness of night.

" You shall be pilot, Teenah, and carry the basket and trunk; Chrissy will take Lulu now from me, and Uncle Dick has more than his back and arms full already. Be wary, and do nothing until you see or hear from me."

He pressed his lips to the brow of his half-sleeping child, whispered a blessing as he laid her softly in the old woman's arms, and turned his footsteps in the direction of home.

The nights are long at Christmas, and morning had not yet broken. Damp and dark the way lay before them; and one who has never traversed a Southern forest can scarcely conceive of its intricacies. Sometimes at the crossings, or where the paths met, Teenah would make the old people sit down with their burdens, while she went alone to reconnoitre, instead of taking the one indicated by either of them. In this way their progress was very

slow; but fortunately they made no diver-·
sions, and the first light of morning found
them well advanced on their way, within half
a mile of their destination. Then for the last
time they sat down to rest, with their faces
turned backward towards the dear old home
they had so strangely forsaken.

" Better gone wid the chilluns when de way
war open," Uncle Dick muttered; then, as if
expecting a reproof from his sterner companion, he added: " Uncle Dick's a fool! He can't
see noffin clar any more."

" Look away yonder," said Teenah, starting
suddenly to her feet and indicating the direction with her finger; "dar's fire up de river!
Don't you see dat clar, Uncle Dick?"

Poor old Dick groaned aloud. "'Tis at de
plantation," he said; " and poor Mar's Alfred
will be slewed like de wild beast by grillas.
Let me crawl my ole limbs back and die wid
him, Chrissy?"

" Hush such nonsense, ole man! Some people
has no head, and dat's de fault I find wid our

color. Who but Aunt Chrissy rocked him in his cradle, and would die now fur to save him? But we's udder things to do now, Dick! Here's de chile's mouth to fill, and the chile's tender heart to comfort, while our own chilluns has gone out free, bress de good Lord!"

The fire was evidently at the plantation; and by the way it spread and grew brighter, there was little doubt that the buildings were all lighted.

"I see plainly who is at de bottom of it all," said old Chrissy. " 'Tis dem dar triflin' young men who offer to hunt de runaways. Ole Mar's McIntosh best to send his own son to de army when he talk so bery loud bout patrotism."

" De grillas mostly no account, white trash," responded Dick. " Dey need Mar's Fred to 'vise um whar to strike. De ole man's money helps de young man's wit right smart."

Uncle Dick was as shrewd a philosopher and reasoned as soundly as Dickens when he said: " Patent-boots, lemon-colored kid gloves, and a fur coat-collar, assist jokes materially."

For some time the heir of McIntosh Grove had been no favorite at the cottage. The feeblest-minded servant there could discover that his preaching and his practice were at variance. None could talk secession louder than he; but while other young men had taken up arms and joined the insurgents, the eighth month of the war found him still only an idle vindicator of the cause at home. He was on a journey of pressing necessity, so at least it was urged when the first volunteers left the county; then a most unfortunate sprain had disabled his wrist for months; but while the old gentleman's funds were contributed freely, the son's cockade and the son's courage could not be questioned. Rumor said he was in the councils of the guerillas, if not in the camp of the Confederates.

The night walk ended silently and sorrowfully. Little Lulu, after such a night of troubled half-consciousness, awoke in the wretched cabin. Aunt Chrissy had lighted a fire and swung a camp-kettle, not upon the hearth, for the cabin had neither chimney nor hearth, but out beneath a large pine in front of the door. There she made coffee, roasted sweet potatoes and fried bacon, all of which they had brought in their store basket from the plantation. There was a smaller basket of delicacies for Lulu, part of the Christmas-turkey, a glass of jelly, and some cakes; the last, Aunt Chrissy affirmed, which the poor child might see for many a day.

Teenah found a small piece of broken board, which she set up and covered with a napkin. She called it Lulu's table. Upon it the child's first meal was spread in the forest.

CHAPTER VI.

NOTHING could exceed Lulu's surprise on awaking to find herself dressed in such a wild, strange place. She began to cry, when Teenah said: " Isn't it nice, Lulu, to come out yer and see all de pretty birds in de woods, and more flowers dan we **could** ever pull? Uncle Dick is gone to fish for mullet, and we will fish for sheep-heads in de creek. You shall have a little line all to yourself, and when your papa comes can tell him about it."

Such soothing words and promises calmed the wondering child. When breakfast was eaten they went out for a ramble in the pine woods, Teenah forgetting how very weary **and** footsore she was in her efforts to amuse **her** little charge, who was more precious to her **in** her misfortune than ever before.

All the morning they plucked wild flowers, and braided them into wreaths, or listened to the mocking-birds calling to one another from tree to tree, or watched the play of the gay lizards until the sound of something like a horn recalled them to the cabin. Uncle Dick had found an old conch-shell which had been left behind by the cow-hunters, and was trying to get music out of it, for music was the solace of his weary life; and the beloved fiddle had been left on the old shelf at home.

At night the cabin was lighted with pine knots, and they all sat down together upon the rude seats they had constructed, and told stories until Lulu fell asleep in Teenah's arms and was laid upon her little bed. A mosquito curtain was then carefully drawn around her, and Teenah lay down at her feet almost worn out with fatigue and anxiety.

Great was their joy on awaking the next morning to find a familiar friend stretched out on the rough floor beside them. It was dear

faithful old Zack, though how he had discovered their retreat was a mystery to them. He
licked their hands and barked and howled in
answer to their caresses, until Teenah declared
he had gone crazy for joy.

Zack was a noble hound, old and sagacious,
and had long been the especial pet of the
household. He used to accompany the young
mistress in her walks over the plantation, and
she taught him to carry her basket in his
mouth. He had been known to come home
from a hunt with a wounded bird for Lulu;
and once when a cross pig broke into the poul-
try-yard, and swallowed one young chicken,
and bit and lamed another, he took the poor
lame little thing up tenderly in his mouth and
carried it to Aunt Chrissy, knowing full well
she would take care of it. There was another
thing that endeared him more than all the rest
to his master. After the death of the beloved
young Mistress had desolated the cottage, old
Zack was missed from his watch-post on the
piazza; search was made, and the faithful crea-

ture was found stretched beside the new-made grave. For months he held his night-watch there; and not until the lawless guerillas began their depredations did he go back to his old place.

When Alfred Browning returned to his solitary dwelling that night, Zack **met** him with unusual demonstrations, running up and down the piazza and around the house as though there was something to tell. His master followed him, saying: "What is it, old doggy? Tell me what it is, good fellow?"

But though Zack tried hard to tell, and his master followed him closely, nothing was discovered; everything around the premises **was** as silent as death. After examining his pistol to see that it was all right in case of emergency, he threw himself down upon the hall lounge and soon fell asleep.

He was aroused by the barking of the dog. A bright light was shining through the hall window, and a scent of smoke was in the air. Grasping his pistol firmly, he hastened to the door, and discovered flames bursting from a dozen cabins. Old Zack was at his side barking furiously, and the two went together through the gate which led to the negro quarters. Not a person was to be seen; but a shout behind them soon revealed the culprits. Several ill-dressed men stood on the back piazza, seen plainly by the burning pine-knot which one of their number was in the act of applying to the cottage.

With a sudden rush and bound, master and dog cleared the intervening space, and the next instant the torch-bearer fell dead among his comrades. Zack held another of the miscreants fast by the throat, while the trusty revolver felled a third. At that moment a stout negro, armed with a club, rushed from the kitchen and began to deal blows upon the others, who, discharging their pistols as they went, fled through the shrubbery.

One shot took effect in Browning's right arm, wounding it severely. The negro, preserving a rigid silence, ripped open the sleeve, and bound the wounded arm firmly with a handkerchief.

Zack still held his man fast, with the blood streaming from the wound inflicted by his teeth, while his two stout forepaws upon the fellow's breast prevented his efforts to draw his pistol.

"I will take care of him now, Zack," said Browning, in a voice as cool and calm as though nothing unusual had occurred. "Deliver your weapons, coward!"

"I cannot get at 'em," he said, in a strangled tone; "the hound is killing me."

"Serving you right, then! Zack, down, my good fellow!"

The dog obeyed, and the man yielded his knife and pistol.

"I think I know you," continued Browning; "and you are the last man I would have picked out for so dirty a job. How have I injured you, that you would revenge thus?"

"You never done me no injury, Mister Alfred, and it was your blessed wife what took care of my ole mother when she had the misery in her side. I was dead-drunk on your own kin's whiskey when I joined the *Rangers*, as they call themselves. I couldn't bear to go away to camp and leave the ole woman to starve to home."

"So you sold yourself to burn, and plunder, and steal! Once I could have fed your old mother, Jerry; but you have taken my corn, and bacon, and sugar, and driven off my cattle to the camp of the rebels. Not satisfied with that, you would to-night have burned my house above my head. May God forgive you so dastardly an act!"

"On my knees, Mr. Browning, I tell you I didn't have no hand in that first business at all. It was only Christmas-eve I was invited down to the grove to take egg-nog and git a few comforts for the ole woman. I didn't calculate to jine 'um; but yesterday they come and said how my name was on their paper, and I'd got to stand it, or start right straight off for camp."

"If what you say is true, Jerry Wilkes, I forgive you."

A voice from the darkey whispered: "*It is true*, Mar's Alfred."

Browning continued:

"You see, Jerry, I have made bloody work of it. One of your companions lies there dead as a herring; another is badly wounded. Assist me to take him into the house now; then go for a surgeon. No time is to be lost. Saddle Billy and ride in haste, or it may be all over with the villain."

The wounded man was then lifted tenderly, and conveyed to the same soft lounge on which Browning was sleeping an hour before. His groans were painful to listen to, and Jerry was again urged to go quickly for the nearest surgeon.

CHAPTER VII.

"I say, Mar's Alfred, you done 'zactly right not to be too hard on Jerry," said the negro, as the sound of horses' hoofs rattled down the carriage-way towards the public road. "Mar's Fred git de boys drunk as ole debil! I watch 'um."

"How came you here to-night, Tim, just at the time you were wanted?"

"I 'spect mischief, and come to warn ole Dick. When I found him done gone I put on his ole clofes and made myself ole man like him, else dis yer darkey's neck mightn't be warf ony de use ob a halter. Tole you yisday, Mar's Alfred, what to 'spect. De trute is, dey say you is turned abalishoner, and we darkeys gwine to fight for you and ole Linkum."

"I am much obliged to you," said Browning.

" But when you go home now, will you not be suspected ? "

" Look out for dat ar. You know my ooman libs up de riber to ole Gibbses. I ask Miss Ally for pass to go and see Rosa. Dis yer's it. Den I brought round here in time for de fight."

"You are all right, Tim, and a brave fellow."

The surgeon came and dressed the guerilla's wounds, which he pronounced dangerous. Then Browning had his own arm attended to, and advised Jerry to have his neck examined; but he said he had washed away the blood and found it was only a scratch. The truth was, he was too much ashamed of his night's work, and too thankful for his escape, to heed the slight injury he had received.

The wounded man moaned all day long, and Browning sat beside him, wet his lips, and gave him every attention he would have bestowed upon a suffering friend or brother. His first indignation had all passed away, and the lessons of the Good Teacher fell upon his mind with new weight. " But I say unto you, love your enemies : bless **them** that curse you ; do good **to** them that hate **you, and pray for** them that despitefully use you and persecute **you,** that you may be the children **of** your Father which is in Heaven, for He maketh His sun to rise on the evil and the good, and sendeth rain upon the **just** and upon the unjust." It was like a voice from the skies speaking to a heart overburdened with grief.

Jerry had gone away, "just to ease the mind of the old woman," he said, promising **to** return and take care of the wounded man **at** night ; and the faithful watcher and the uncon- scious sufferer were the only human beings in **the cottage.** No one had been near **to** remove the body of the dead man, which was still lying on the piazza where **he** fell. But towards noon a cart came down the avenue and entered the great gate. Two men accompanied it. Zack went to the door, and returned whining to his master, who ordered him **to** be quiet.

9

He understood the order, and lay down beside him contented.

The body' was laid upon straw in the cart, and driven away without a word.

It was drawing towards evening when the injured man opened his eyes for the first time with a look of consciousness. Fastening them upon Browning, he inquired feebly: "Where am I?"

"At Rose Cottage," was the reply.

His eyes closed again, and he remained silent for some time, until his attendant wet his lips, as he had done all day at frequent intervals.

"Are you Alfred Browning?" he asked.

"I am the person you mention."

"Where are the boys?"

"Fled, all but one, who has been carted off."

"Who brought me in here?"

"I helped to do it. You see, with my right arm shot through, I could not do it alone."

"What time is it?"

"Four o'clock in the evening. Are you feeling better?"

"I don't know. I feel like I was dreaming."

He closed his eyes again and murmured to himself indistinctly. Who the poor man was Browning could not tell, but evidently no person who belonged in the vicinity. There was something in his speech which seemed to belie the extreme rusticity of his garb; something, too, in the tone of the voice not wholly strange, and yet he was not sure. Between his own weakness and weariness Browning also felt not very unlike a person in a bewildering dream.

CHAPTER VIII.

JERRY came back that night as he promised, and assumed the care of the wounded guerilla, insisting that Browning should go away and get some sleep.

He went away, but not to sleep. He went forth into the fresh evening air, and stood amid the ashes of his burnt cabins. Not a log of them remained; only the stable, kitchen, and cottage had escaped the conflagration, and these had been saved almost by a miracle. Was it likely, he asked himself, that his enemies would be satisfied with their last night's work, and leave him thenceforward in peace? Could his little, motherless child be safe again in their once happy home? He knew too well the unscrupulous character of the men he had to contend with to believe it. That brand of *abolitionism* meant persecution to the death.

But Alfred Browning was not an abolitionist. His belief in slavery was hereditary, and he had never cared to question it. It came from a long line of ancestors, all slave-owners. In a moral point of view, no merit beyond that of patriotism could be attached to his enfranchisement of his servants. He loved his country truly, the whole of it more than a section ; and there was no power on earth which could force him to raise a weapon against it.

Musing upon the sad uncertainty of the future, his steps followed unconsciously the well-worn footpath to his wife's grave. Silence and peace brooded over it with wings like a dove. No jar of earthly discord would evermore disturb the beloved sleeper. "Better thus," he sighed, "than to have tarried longer here. In your own saintly footsteps, my darling, lead the little one and me to your heavenly rest!"

For nearly an hour he sat absorbed in silent meditation. Old Zack was beside him, with one paw resting upon the grave, and the other upon his master's knee, looking intelligently into his face.

"You have not forgotten her," his master said, breaking the long silence with a caress as he rose to depart. "Nothing can forget her. Come, my good dog; I must send you to Lulu."

They went back through the orangery. The fruit was just ripening, and he plucked the fairest he could discover in the dim light of evening. These were carried into the cottage and put into one of Lulu's little baskets. They then left the house again, and Browning took the same path which he had taken the night before. Zack ran with his nose to the earth, snuffing the air until he caught the track, when he barked joyfully.

"You have found it, have you?" said his master. "Take the basket, then, and go. Be careful, and don't spill."

The dog opened his jaws for the trust, and bounded away. Early the next morning Aunt Chrissy found him at the cabin door with his basket; a sure token that, whatever else might have happened at the plantation, the master was safe.

The children ate the oranges with their breakfast, talking all the while to the dog as though they had not seen him for a month.

"When is papa coming?" asked Lulu; "and why did he send us away from the pretty home?"

Zack couldn't tell, but jumped and barked as loudly as he could; and his coming made Lulu happy all day.

That same day the wounded man lay dying at the cottage. His injury proved too severe for the skill of the surgeon or the care of his kind attendant. All night he wandered in mind, and towards morning appeared to be sinking. Jerry was dispatched again for the physician, who said at a glance there was no hope. The poor stranger was dying unrecognised, if not uncared for.

"I think, Jerry," said Browning, when they were alone again, "that you know more of this man than you are inclined to tell. If he has friends in the neighborhood, it should be our duty to inform them of his condition."

"We took a black oath to keep mum, sir. This man, 'specially, didn't wish to be found out in such a business. He's ben gone away from these parts for many years, and got right smart rich, they say, down in Texas. He jus' run down here to see his sister, on his way to join the army. You know'd him when you was both boys, I reckon. I ain't seen him since he turned fifer and run away to Mexico to the war, more'n sixteen years ago."

"Ah, Jack Thomas, my old school-fellow! I remember him well," said Browning. "And a brave boy he was, too!"

"A leetle bit rapscallious, Jack was! Liked *adventurin'* better'n buttered hominy, and could be put up to a'most anything, just as they put him up to this yer work, which was none of his own planning."

"Tell me how it all happened, Jerry. I must know!"

" Well, then, Jack's mother's died, you know, since he's went away, and his sister's married and gone down to St. Mary's to live. He brought up to the Grove Christmas evening, just as the boys was drinking their egg-nog and getting merry. Mr. Fred was mighty glad to see him, and said he'd come in the very nick o' time, as there was some fun on the carpet, a—abolition nest to break up (beggin' your pardon, Mister Alfred, them's his very words). He said the boys would do all the dirty work, and wanted a leader; just such a bold Texan ranger as he was, and one whom nobody around there would be likely to know. You know Mister Fred couldn't do nothin' hisself but make egg-nog on account of that lame wrist; and when the men had drunk enough, they was ready to agree to anything. There was ten on 'em all, lettin' alone the new-comer and myself, who wasn't one on 'em and never meant to be. They was to meet in the nigger chapel the next night at midnight; but when the time come, more'n half on 'em was off some-

10

wheres else plundering cattle, which brings better pay than burning housens, and don't sound so bad neither.

" After waitin' to the chapel more'n an hour, some was in favor of backin' straight out like the rest had done; but Mister Fred said right off: 'No! Let two men go up and reconnoitre, and if everything was quiet like, there was men enough there to do the job.' So two of the boys set out, and when they come back reported there wasn't a soul on the whole premises. Every man, ooman, and child was gone off to the Union folks. Nothing was left on the plantation but a dog and two horses.

" By this time we'd all took drink enough to git mighty high. Jack changed his fine broadcloth for a coarse rig, and we started. You know how it ended; and ef some folks had got shot in place of Jack Thomas, 'twouldn't seemed to be much matter. Jack never knowed he was coming to injure an old acquaintance."

" Poor fellow! Did my uncle know anything about the project, Jerry?"

"Not to my mind, Mr. Alfred. Madam and him and the young ladies drove away in the carriage in the afternoon. The old gentleman is death to the bone on abolitionists; but I don't think, let him talk as he will, he'd be as hard agin his own kin as the young one."

Browning thought, what he had quite too fine a sense of propriety to utter, that his cousin owed him an old grudge. He knew he had never in his heart forgiven him for winning the hand of Ellen Hunter; and although, at the time, his words of congratulation had been as loud as the loudest, they had never appeared to him to be sincere.

CHAPTER IX.

AT noon a visitor arrived at the cottage. It was Ally McIntosh, looking just as pretty and blooming as when we first met her in New Hampshire half-a-dozen years ago. She said they had that morning returned from a visit to her sister at Spring Lake. They heard of the fire on their way, and she had heard some other things from the servants since their arrival home. Would Cousin Alfred be good enough to tell her all about it?

He was frank enough to tell her the truth as far as he understood it, leaving her to make her own inferences. She listened with flushed cheeks and tearful eyes.

"Just as I expected," she said, stamping her foot impatiently. "I quarrel for you, Cousin Alfred, every day, and would help you if I

could. Fred is a grand coward, and has
proved it now more clearly than ever before.
You did not say it, but I know he is at the
bottom of all this; and Tim knows it too. If
he doesn't just march off to camp now, I'll tell
father every word about it, and all the world
besides! His wrist is no more lame than mine
is, and never has been! Fred is a sneak, and
I am ashamed of him."

At the close of this tempest of words, Ally
burst into tears. Her cousin strove to comfort her.

"I say, Cousin Alfred, I cannot help crying
when I am so indignant. If I were a man I
suppose I should swear. It was bad enough
to hear you called an abolitionist every day,
and dear Cousin Ellen accused of being your
teacher; but who ever thought of a McIntosh
condescending to counsel with thieves and rob-
bers! They say you shot one or two of the
rascals; I wish in my heart you had made a
clean job of it. If I had been near I would
have helped you. Did I understand you, you

had one of the wounded wretches on your hands?"

"Come in, Ally, and see."

She pulled a cluster of white roses from the trellis, and followed him through the hall into the back parlor, where the sufferer had been removed. The physician and Jerry Wilkes were both with him. He had had a morning of intense suffering, but it was almost over. He recognised Browning, who spoke to him kindly, and asked him if he had any wish to communicate.

"To be buried beside my good mother," he replied feebly; "and don't let my sister know I met such a fool's death. It would break her heart."

Noticing Ally for the first time now, he asked:

"Is that Mary? She looks like an angel. She was a little child when I left home—a dear little child!"

His mind wandered again. He was away in Mexico, fighting over his battles there, huzzaing for the old flag, and planting it on the heights of Chapultepec.

"'Tis hard work, comrade," he said, addressing himself to Browning, who stood supporting his head; "but then we are bound to win."

Cold drops of perspiration were on his forehead, and a blueness was creeping over his lips. The doctor felt his pulse, and whispered Browning to lead his cousin from the room. Neither spoke as they went, but Ally wept as though her heart would burst.

Death is a most eloquent preacher of human brotherhood. No matter how widely different our earthly interests, or how far removed our earthly lot, by this one token, "*Dust thou art, and unto dust shalt thou return,*" are we the children of the same common parent on earth, and the same Father in heaven.

"It always seemed to me that men who would engage in infamous acts must be scoundrels or barbarians," said Ally, after an interval of silence. "Whatever that man may have done, he doesn't look as though meant for either."

"He was a noble fellow by nature, Ally, and would perhaps have been such with other influences; but poor, and proud, and father-less, has led many a high spirit into error. The poor fellow had to jostle his way in the world, and with unscrupulous men has grown unscrupulous. I feel no resentment towards him. The greater guilt lies elsewhere."

"Fred shall come and see what he has done," responded Ally, with spirit; "and the man shall be buried decently. I can promise father for that."

"You may promise *me* for that. I claim the privilege of laying him by his mother."

"Cousin Alfred, I have not seen Lulu!"

"I have sent her away to a place of safety. The contest may not yet be over. They are filling another regiment in the county, you know."

"That *arm* will free you now, cousin."

"I ask no such exemption. My *principles*

will for ever prevent me from taking arms against my country."

Ally's horse and servant stood waiting at the gate. Her cousin assisted her to mount, and she rode slowly and sorrowfully away through the pine woods which lay between the two plantations. Before reaching home she met her father, a handsome, grey-haired man, who sat in his saddle with all the ease and grace of youth. He, too, had heard of the tragic events at the cottage, and was riding over to satisfy himself of the truth. Probably his own conscience was not quite easy on the subject ; for, though he would have scorned such measures as his son had adopted, he had not been sparing in his epithets and denunciation of his more loyal nephew.

Ally was glad to meet him, and, sending the servant forward, she gave free expression to her feelings.

" Go, and look for yourself," she said at last. " See the cabins all in ashes, the store-houses emptied and burned, and the family fled in

11

terror. Worse than all this, behold a stranger deceived unto death. I tell you, father, I blush to bear the name of McIntosh, for my brother is both a villain and a coward."

"You are fatigued and excited, my daughter! Go home and repose yourself, and I will see how affairs stand at the cottage."

"I will tell you, sir, what must be done immediately. Tim must be sent to prepare the body of the stranger for burial, as no soul is there to do a thing, except that booby of a Jerry Wilkes, who looks as ashamed as a dog that has been hung and cut down. Then a messenger must be dispatched to St. Mary's for the poor fellow's sister. Oh, sir, if you had only heard him speak of his sister, and beg she might never be told of the way in which he came to his death! Two men must also go and dig a grave beside the widow Thomas, for he asked to be buried close to his good old mother."

"Poor Jack," said her father, brushing away a tear. "Do everything you like, Ally."

"There is another thing that must be done, sir, before the week closes," and she dropped her voice and spoke huskily ; "*Fred must go to camp*, or, as little sympathy as I have for the cause, I will put on his clothes and go myself for the honor of the family. I give you warning, father ; and you know I never have spoken falsely."

He regarded her for a moment without reply, then lifted his hat and bowed as they parted. Every vestige of color had fled from the proud man's face ; he was pale as ashes.

CHAPTER X.

The burial took place the next morning. The few neighbors who had known the widow Thomas and her children were apprised, and assembled to follow the young man to his grave. The McIntosh carriage followed the hearse with the afflicted sister, but Fred was nowhere in the procession. He had started for the army that morning, and his arrival was chronicled in the Savannah papers the next week as "*another patriot in the field.*"

At the close of the burial service, Ally and her father both urged Browning to go home with them to dinner, but he would not be persuaded. Solitude and a ruined home were more congenial to his feelings than the society of faithless friends or false kindred. Since the avowal of his union sentiments, he had been

painfully aware that, with one exception, he had
not a single friend at the Grove, where he had
once been as a son of the house. His aunt
and two youngest cousins were rabid secession-
ists, and during the last months of his wife's
life had treated her with a coldness as marked
as their former intimacy. Only Ally had clung
to her to the last, like a good, loving sister, and
been true to her memory.

The cottage looked desolate enough as
Browning approached it. He had grown a
little accustomed to the loss of his wife's tender
greeting, but Lulu's joyous welcome and sweet
kisses had never been wanting before. He
almost expected to see her now, with her light
footsteps and sunny curls, running from the
piazza to meet him. It was the first time within
his recollection he had ever alighted to open
his own gate. Usually half-a-dozen sable children had rushed from the cabins at his approach,
equally happy to catch a word or a penny
from the indulgent master. "Would they be
better off now," he asked himself, "in their

new condition of freedom?" He hoped so, but feared otherwise. It was an experiment—a dangerous one, he thought, too—for the African.

A well known bark interrupted his reverie, and Zack bounded forth to meet him with such expressions of joy as brought tears to his eyes. He tied Billy in the stable, then walked to the house, caressing the dog as he went.

Lulu's little basket was on the piazza, with something within wrapped carefully. He unfolded the napkin, and found a nicely broiled bird, a piece of corn-cake, and a sheepshead, to which was attached a yellow leaf, pencilled in Teenah's rude letters, "Lulu sends papa a fish she hooked in de creek."

Browning had scarcely tasted food since Christmas morning. He had refrained, not from the want of it, but from a sense of loathing. The bird and fish, and, more than all, Lulu's sweet little message, now acted as appetizers. He placed them on the uncleared Christmas table, brought a bottle of claret from the vault, and sat down to his solitary meal.

For the first time he noticed Aunt Chrissy's rude attempts at decoration. Branches of cedar, pine, and holly were green in the windows, and great boughs of pomegranate, with their drooping scarlet bells, hung from the ceiling. There were two or three vases of flowers on the table, but, although withered, it was evident that the inartistic hand of the faithful Chrissy had no part either in their selection or arrangement. Only the child Teenah had thus caught her mistress's art of blending hues. Those half-withered flowers bore his thoughts away to his lost love. It was almost a pleasure to him now to think that her feet were straying amid the flowers that grow in the fields of immortality.

Only the Christmas before, he remembered she told him, " *To be with Christ* would be better even than the celebration of His blessed advent." He did not understand her then, but thought some cloud was resting on her mind. Now he knew it was not a cloud, but the sunshine of glory; a foretaste of the fulness of joy and rest which remain for the saints of the Lord.

"Blessed are the dead which die in the Lord.

"They shall hunger no more, neither thirst any more; neither shall the sun light on them, nor any heat. For the Lamb which is in the midst of the throne shall feed them, and shall lead them unto living fountains of water; and God shall wipe away all tears from their eyes.

"There shall be no more death, neither sorrow nor crying; neither shall there be any more pain, for the former things are passed away."

CHAPTER XI.

THAT evening little Lulu's basket was filled with oranges and cakes, and old Zack sent forth again on his now well known way. His master would gladly have retained the faithful creature, but he had no other messenger, and Lulu's comfort and happiness were more to him than any other consideration. But for her his own life would have been to him of little value, bereft as it was of everything that makes life desirable. No star of hope gleamed for him in the misty future. He could discern no light of peace for his rent and distracted country. "Greek had met Greek" in terrible conflict, and rivers of kindred blood must flow. War appeared to him a relic of barbarism. He would not fight willingly, and, if

12

forced to do so, never on the side which he regarded as wrong.

That night passed quietly. The next morning he armed himself, and went out as he had been accustomed to do since the warning was given him that his services were required in the Confederate army. A press-gang had already taken one man from the county as adverse to the rebel cause as himself. He would elude it if possible; if not, his purpose was fixed to resist unto death.

All that day he passed in the forest, shooting nothing, though game was abundant. At nightfall he found a shelter, where he remained until nearly midnight, then sought his desolated home again.

Softly as his footsteps fell on the sandy paths, they aroused a watchful listener, and before he reached the cottage door Tim was standing on the piazza to meet him. The unexpectedness of this meeting startled him for a moment, and he cocked his pistol.

"Don't shoot, Mar's Alfred! Nobody yer

but Tim. De coast am clar for de rest of de night sure. You 'scaped 'um."

" Escaped whom, Tim? "

"De 'cruitin' sargent and his no-account trash. I 'spected dey might be round some-whars, and got anodder permit to go and see Rosa."

" Have they been here to-night? "

" Just gone, Mar's Alfred."

" Where were you, Tim? "

" Hid under de peazzar steps. I come yer before dark, and didn't like to go way without seein' you. Was feared you might hab trouble agin and need one ob Tim's big club. Wouldn't mind shakin' daylight out ob dat sort ob white trash no more'n Zack minds shakin' 'possum. Hearn ebery word dey said, Mar's Alfred! Dey's powerful full ob patrotism, and want you mighty bad to help drive dem dar abolishoners way from de coast."

" Who were they? "

" Didn't know 'em, sir. Ony two, tree Mar's Fred's grillas wid 'em. Dey talk like dey's great men somewhar. One ob de grillas said dey might as well finish up de job de boys begin Christmas night; but de yaller-striped man said, ' 'Twould neber do to 'stroy de trap afore dey cotch de rat. Dey be sartin' to find him in't some time, and cotch him too, and make a cap'en on him.' Dey gwine to set a watch for you to-morrow, Mar's Alfred, and ebery day."

Browning was silent for a few minutes, then said, "I wish to make Cousin Ally a present of Daisy, Tim. It was her father's first gift to Miss Ellen, and I know she will like the gentle creature for *her* sake. Her saddle, bridle, and whip are in the stable loft."

" Yis, sir! I lead her home wid me."

" And, Tim, there is one thing more. If you get time, or happen to be going that way, just tell Aunt Chrissy not to get uneasy about me, but to wait patiently until she sees or hears something further. My business in Florida may detain me some little time. You may tell her to hope for good news."

Browning then threw himself upon his bed, and was soon sleeping soundly and peacefully. At early dawn he was awakened by the faithful Tim.

"Mar's Alfred, 'tis time you is up and gwine. I've done saddled Daisy, and Billy too. Dar's hot coffee in de kitchen! I make it strong to keep me wake."

"I thought **you** went home hours ago, Tim!"

"Didn't go home, sir! Couldn't leave you, Mar's Alfred. 'Fraid you sleep too long, and git cotched. Promised Miss Ally to keep good look for you."

"Go bring me the largest saddle-bags! I may need some changes of clothing."

Before it was fairly light, the doors of Rose Cottage were locked fast, the stables empty, and the master on his way to the nearest ford.

It was not the first time Billy had swum the boundary river, and he plunged in without a fear, and in a few minutes **was** shaking the **water** from his flanks on the Florida shore.

"Farewell for the present to Georgia misrule!" exclaimed Browning. "I am an alien until better times. Whenever the hour comes that I can strike boldly for my native State, if God spares my life, I will stand amid her loyal sons. But the rod of the usurper must first be broken."

CHAPTER XII.

WHILE the fugitive was riding leisurely towards Jacksonville, little Lulu and Teenah were trying their best to catch him some fine fish. Uncle Dick had taken plenty of mullet in his net the day before, but the children believed what Browning had written in the little note which he put in Zack's basket— that the fish relished much better because Lulu caught it.

After angling some time unsuccessfully, they went to another place where the water was stiller and deeper. Teenah held the line very steadily, and presently a large perch began to nibble at the fiddler upon the hook. The fiddler is a very minute species of crab, found in great abundance on the Southern sea-coast, as well as on the margins of creeks and rivers where the tide water sets back. There is no bait of which perch and sheepshead are so fond. The mullet is' not caught with a hook, as it never bites. It is a species of sucker, and has to be drawn in a seine or net.

"Look! look!" exclaimed Lulu, in a whisper. "One, two, three fat sheepshead coming to drive away the perch. They all want fiddler for breakfast."

Teenah began to draw in the line.

"Dat perch is fairly hooked, Lulu! Soft, now! pull steadily. 'Tis a beauty."

In a few minutes more, one of the sheepshead was lying with the perch in their basket, and they were delighted. Lulu said those were a plenty for one morning, and Zack should carry them to papa as soon as Aunt Chrissy could dress and broil them.

So the children ran joyfully back to the cabin, and Aunt Chrissy baked a fresh corn-cake in the ashes and broiled the fish. Then Zack was started off, with many loving messages from Lulu to darling papa.

It takes but little to make or mar the happiness of childhood, and all that day Lulu went around as happy as any bird, thinking of her father's pleasure at sight of old Zack and the basket.

When night came, and Teenah had heard her little prayer, and drawn the white mosquito net around her bed, she said: "Good night, Teenah! Zacky will be back in the morning. Wake me early."

The dog did not come. · When Lulu awoke, her first inquiry was for him. Aunt Chrissy said:

"Don't fret, chile, about it. De ole dog will be sure to come some time wid plenty of oranges for Honey."

Lulu could not be persuaded to go into the pine woods for flowers that morning, nor down to the creek to fish, for fear she would miss Zack; and when she had eaten her dinner, and taken her customary nap, and he did not come, she was ready to cry for disappointment. Teenah said they would go and meet him.

13

So all the afternoon they lingered in the paths they knew he would take; but when the sun went down they had to go back to the cabin without him.

Uncle Dick felt very sorry for Lulu. He took her upon his knee, wiped away her tears, and said, "he 'spected Mar's Alfred wanted Zack hisself to go huntin' wid him, and keep off de wicked bars and tiger-cats." Then when she was soothed he sang over and over, "Boun' fur de kingdom, will you go to glory wid me?" until she fell asleep and forgot her grief.

Two days more passed, and Zack had not been seen at the cabin. Aunt Chrissy shook her head ominously when she thought no one saw her, and scolded Uncle Dick every time he ventured to hint at anything being wrong. Lulu never spoke another word about the dog, but asked a great many questions about *bears* and *tiger-cats*, and whether they lived in the swamps.

The third night, after she was asleep, footsteps were heard approaching the cabin. Uncle Dick ventured out cautiously, and was delighted to find Tim, who had not been able to fulfil his promise sooner. He had a bag of sweet potatoes on his back, and a small sack of hominy in his arms, and came puffing and panting under the double burden.

"Come in yer wid ye!" said Aunt Chrissy, overjoyed at sight of a human being in their solitude. "De poor chile is sleepin' thar like a lamb. How is all?"

"De cottage am standing, Chrissy, but de rest am mostly burned clean and clar."

"How is young Massar?"

"Mar's Alfred done gone away to 'scape de *press-gangers*. Don't 'stress yourself so 'bout it. He tole me fur to tell you dar'd be good news fur you 'fore long. Keep quiet and pray de Lord."

Tim then recounted, in his own quaint fashion, all that had occurred since the night they left the plantation, not forgetting his part in the deadly conflict with the guerillas.

It was a picture worthy of a painter, that rude cabin away in the lonely forest, with the dark group within, clustered together in one corner, as seen by the dim light of a pine-knot torch which old Dick held in his trembling hand. The little bed, with its white curtain festooned every day with fresh flowers, was altogether in shadow.. Teenah had forsaken her blanket at Lulu's feet and joined the group. Tim sat there hour after hour answering all the questions of the old people, and promising to keep them informed of every event of interest in the future.

Teenah asked but one question, whether her master took Zack with him? When informed he did not, she said, "If the guerillas had killed him, it would almost break Lulu's heart."

Tim said he would go back by way of the cottage and see if he could find him; but there was no necessity for his doing so. While they were speaking they heard a scratch at the door of the cabin, followed by a low howl. Dick

said it was a black wolf; but Teenah's ears
were not deceived.

"'Tis ole Zack hisself!" she said joyfully.
" Open quick ; he may be hurt!"

Uncle Dick was still afraid, but Tim opened
the door, and the dog entered silently with his
basket in his mouth. He made no demonstrations of joy when Teenah threw her arms
around him and caressed him, but put down
his basket, and stretched himself out as if
quite exhausted.

" Poor ole fellow! He is starved," Aunt
Chrissy said, and went for a piece of corn-
cake.

He would not eat, but licked Teenah's hands
and cried mournfully. They thought he was
hurt, but on examination found neither wound
nor bruise.

" Let me look in his basket," said Teenah,
holding it up to the light of the pine-knot.
" Everything is just as we sent it. Nothing
is de matter ob him, ony he wants to tell us he
couldn't find his master."

CHAPTER XIII.

TEENAH was right. Three whole days Zack lingered around the premises, sometimes lying at his old watch-post on the piazza, sometimes going to the empty stables or barking at the kitchen door; but he could nowhere find the object of his search, no one to caress him as usual, or give him food. When quite exhausted with fasting, he took up his basket again, and returned to the cabin. It was very fortunate that Tim was there before him, otherwise his coming would have occasioned serious alarm for the safety of the beloved master.

When the dog had rested awhile, Teenah offered him food again. He ate but little, then went and lay down before Lulu's bed, where she discovered him in the morning as soon as she awoke. But Zack was not happy.

He would only follow the children silently when they called him, liking better to lie in the shadow of the cabin. Teenah told Lulu, if they could only make him understand her father was safe, he would be as lively as ever.

Many long days passed with no change and little interest, except an occasional night visit from Tim, who brought the old folks tobacco and meal, and told them all the news he could learn. Four of Col. McIntosh's negroes had run away to the coast, and two of old Gibb's. The Union folks had whipped the Georgia and Florida boys at Fernandina, and were blockading the St. John's below Jacksonville; all of which was very good news to them, since the Unionists were believed to be the *particular friends of the darkeys.*

"Ef we could ony hear from young massar and de chilluns, 'twould be de greatest comfort," Aunt Chrissy said, as they sat smoking together in the doorway one warm evening. "Dar must be bad work on de coast, whar we hear de big guns so much!"

But weeks passed with no news either from the master or his old servants. Lulu cried herself to sleep every night, and Teenah had hard work to keep her cheerful through the day. Uncle Dick became more and more querulous, and while his wife scolded him as often as ever, her own faith in the future began to grow dim. Teenah was the only one habitually cheerful; and she sang hymns, imitated the birds, played with old Zack, or braided wreaths for Lulu from morning until night. Their books had all been left behind, except one little Testament her mistress had given her and taught her to read. She tried to teach Lulu from this, but the child wanted her own pretty books with bright pictures, and would not spell the words in the hard Testament. She wanted her doll, too, and her games and puzzles, and begged Uncle Dick every day to carry her back to her good home. It was getting harder and harder to please the delicate child.

One warm day in early spring, when the bay-flowers were budding in the thickets, and the children had gone in quest of them, old Zack, who had never been quite himself since his last visit to the cottage, came bounding into the cabin, where Aunt Chrissy sat smoking alone. He barked in his old way, put his paws upon her shoulders, then ran out of the door as if to meet some one. Thinking it was the children, she did not move or take her pipe from her mouth until she saw a tall figure standing in the open doorway. Had a ghost appeared to her she could not have stared more wildly; and not until the apparition spoke to her, and called her "*Mother*," did she open her mouth.

"'Tis my own chile!" she said then, rising and clasping him in her arms; "my baby boy dat I sent forth to freedom. He has come to look at ole daddy and mammy once more."

"Come fur to take you 'way wid him," he replied; "de chilluns all dyin' to see thar mother."

Aunt Chrissy shook her head, and said solemnly: "My own flesh and blood mus'n't

14

tempt me to do wrong. I have de precious charge to keep for poor young massar!"

"Mar's Alfred sent me, and give me dis yer fur Teenah," taking a little note from the toe of his brogan.

"Bress de Lord, and blow de conch for Uncle Dick!" Aunt Chrissy exclaimed, quite beside herself with joy when she saw the note. "Poor ole man! how he has mourned for de chilluns, and broke his heart for de chilluns' chillun. Tell him softly, Bona, or he'll go give way."

At the sound of the shell, Teenah and Lulu, as well as old Dick, hurried home to the cabin. They all understood it to be a return call, it having been agreed, if anything happened, to sound the conch. Great was their surprise to meet Bona, and greater their joy when they learned his errand.

Teenah was the only one who could read writing, and it took her a long while to spell out all the words of the note, while Lulu sat down by her side, trying hard to be patient.

The two old folks were weeping together over Bona, whom they never expected to meet again.

"We must start to-night," Teenah said at last. "We must take de warm blankets and shawls, and something to eat on de journey, dat's all we must take. We must travel in de night, and stop in de daytime to rest. Three nights will bring us into de Union lines. We must all take de very best care of Lulu until she gets to Mar's Alfred. Dat's all he said."

Bona said, while they were making ready, he must have one more look at *the old home*, and Uncle Dick whispered to him softly, so Aunt Chrissy might not hear, "Ef he could fihd it dar, to bring de ole fiddle wid him; he missed it so much, and de chilluns would want to hear de ole tunes he used to play dem. He left it on de kitchen shelf, ef de grillas hadn't found it."

There was not much to do except to bake what corn-meal they had into cakes for the journey. The few potatoes left of Tim's sup-

ply they would roast by the way as they
needed them. They had no coffee, and only a
handful of parched rice, which had been their
substitute.

The little bed was left in the corner, robbed
of its blankets and curtains. They could not
carry it so far. Beneath the bed, Teenah lifted
a loose board, and took out the little trunk her
master had intrusted to her care, and then they
were ready to go.

CHAPTER XIV.

THEY left the old cabin in the first dusk of evening. Bona had a boat waiting for them at the mouth of the creek, and they floated down the river until towards morning, when they landed on the Florida side. They remained concealed in the woods during the day, and at night set forward again on foot, keeping their way by the light of the stars, through the heavy pine forests, unmindful of fatigue or danger. The third morning found them on a low, sandy point on the banks of the St. John's. Bona said, if no boat was waiting for them there, they were to signal the first vessel that came down the river.

Uncle Dick was afraid that by so doing they would fall into the hands of the rebels; but Bona assured him no *secesher* dared be seen on the river since the big fleet had gone up. All the vessels that went up or came down were *Union*.

After resting awhile, they built a fire on the sand and cooked breakfast, for they were very hungry after the long night-walk. They had only one corn-cake left in their basket, and half-a-dozen sweet potatoes; but Bona went in search of crabs and came back soon with plenty. These were put into the fire with the potatoes, and when roasted made an excellent meal.

Aunt Chrissy steeped the last grains of her parched rice, and said " thar store held out all de way LIKE DE WIDOW CRUZA'S OIL! We shall cross dis Jurdin to-day, and to-morrow be in de promised land."

Simple believers! To the wandering Israelite, Canaan was not more cloudless than that untried land of freedom to Uncle Dick and Aunt Chrissy, where Mar's Alfred and " de chilluns" awaited them. Snatches of triumphant hymns burst from their lips, the sound of which made little Lulu's heart leap for joy. They were all children together as they sat there on the sandy beach that morning, and Teenah's was the only thoughtful-looking face among them. She had no father to go to like Lulu, no kindred! She was free, but had no home. Lulu's home would be hers for a time until she no longer needed her tender care; and what then? Had the world a welcome for such as she? She was afraid of the great world, where she must walk defenceless and helpless, and sometimes felt, when her thoughts peered into the misty future, as though she would like to creep back to the grave of her beloved mistress, and die.

It was only when the others were so full of joy and hope that such thoughts possessed Teenah's mind. When the cabin was dark, and Uncle Dick and Aunt Chrissy most despondent, when Lulu wailed all day for her papa and the pretty home, then her songs were loudest, for she was making music for others. Now they were all too happy to heed whether she were sad or joyful.

Teenah had a more reflective mind than most children, especially those of her own class. Whether she had any memories earlier than her memories of Rose Cottage is uncertain. Sometimes she used to tell Aunt Chrissy she saw a country in her sleep, warmer and brighter than theirs, where the people were all black, and wore much gold. Some one waved palm-leaves over her there, just as she waved a fan over Lulu when she put her to sleep.

Aunt Chrissy told her it was a dream. It may be her lonely childhood favored such dreams, and that her natural disposition inclined her to solitude, otherwise she would more frequently have been found joining the wild sports of the plantation children. The many hours she spent with her mistress certainly increased the reflective tendency of her mind, and the little knowledge which was imparted to her awakened the wildest thirst for more. She had done all she could to instruct Lulu, and she often queried whether, *now she was free,* she might not be allowed to learn lessons with her when she came to have books and teachers. She knew well no slave-child could be thus privileged. Teenah had no suspicion that her mistress had provided for her education if she remained with Lulu. Had she known it her tender care of the child could not have been increased.

Breakfast had not long been eaten when a little cloud of smoke was observed rising above the river. Teenah was the first to notice it and point it out to the others. They all said it was a steamboat and must be coming down the river, as no vessel had gone up since their arrival at the point, nearly two hours before. It was a long time getting in sight, and sometimes, when the smoke disappeared for a moment, they were ready to believe they had been mistaken, and that no boat was approaching. Then the light vapory cloud would be seen again nearer than before.

After awhile the heavy strokes of the engine were heard, and the puffing of steam; and soon a large three-masted vessel rounded a

15

point not far distant. It was unlike any boat ever seen on the St. Mary's. Bona told them it was a war-vessel and carried great cannon.

A white flag was fastened to Uncle Dick's staff, and Bona held it up and shouted when the gunboat drew nearer. Lulu was much excited, holding fast to Teenah with one hand while the other waved her little handkerchief, as Aunt Chrissy directed.

"They mightn't be willin' to stop for no-account pussons like we are!" she said, "but no one would be hard-hearted enough to leave a tender young chile like her."

The vessel gave signs of halting, and pretty soon a boat was let down by ropes, and half-a-dozen stout men jumped in and pulled for the shore. It was no unusual thing for the gunboats, in their passage up and down the river, to be hailed by fugitives, and their signals were seldom unheeded.

It was not many minutes before the whole party had reached the vessel, and were waiting to climb up the steep sides. When the Captain saw Lulu, he came down the ladder into the boat, took her in his own arms very tenderly, and returned to the vessel with her. Old Zack sprang after her at one leap, to the great amusement of the sailors, who were looking on.

"Please help Teenah, now!" Lulu said naively, addressing the Captain. "Teenah is my nurse, and could never get up those bad steps like Zacky."

Teenah was soon up the ladder at her side; then the Captain took them down into his cabin, brought cologne to bathe Lulu's sunburnt cheeks, and rang for the steward to bring them something nice to eat. The child's black dress and artless story touched his feelings, and he promised to help her find her papa when his vessel reached Fernandina.

CHAPTER XV.

FERNANDINA is built on a low, sandy island on the extreme north-eastern coast of Florida. It was named from a wealthy Spanish resident, Fernandez. The city is built on the eastern or ocean side of the island of Amelia, and was of little importance before the construction of the peninsula railroad, which connects the Atlantic with the Gulf-shore. Since that event it has grown rapidly, and was, at the outbreak of the rebellion, the principal *entrepôt* for the cotton, rice, and sugar of Eastern and Middle Florida. After its occupation by the Union forces, it became a point of some military importance to the North.

The principal wharf of the town was thronged with men on the arrival of the steamer from the St. John's; soldiers, sailors,

and civilians, Anglo-Saxon and African, fra-
ternizing in a common cause, and moved by
common curiosity. The Captain had taken the
children on deck again, and placed them in a
position where they could look over the ship's
sides and amuse themselves by observing objects on shore. Zack posted himself beside
them like a trusty sentinel, while Uncle Dick
and Aunt Chrissy, nearly dumb with astonishment, stood leaning over the gunwale near by.

There was one person amid the crowd on
shore, who gathered in all these familiar objects
at a glance, and whose heart swelled with silent
thanksgiving at the sight. It was little Lulu's
father, waiting and watching for his child.
No vessel had gone up the river the day pre-
vious, otherwise he would have been at the
place appointed to meet them. But Bona was
trusty, and had followed his instructions to the
letter; and, when the vessel touched the pier
Browning's feet were among the first to cross
the plank.

The joy of the meeting may be better imagined than described. Lulu laughed and cried in her father's arms; the two old people wept like children at sight of Mar's Alfred, and Bona grinned with pride and complacency at the success of his adventure, while Zack barked his joy in a most boisterous manner. Teenah alone was silent and undemonstrative. With kind words for others, whenever they had need of them, she had never a syllable for the expression of her own joy or sorrow. Her emotions appeared to have no natural outlet except in singing.

After thanking the Captain for his kindness to Lulu, Browning took his family to the quarters he had provided for them in the city. A number of the old plantation servants were there, clinging to the master still, though free; others had gone to Port Royal and Beaufort in search of employment.

A gentleman came to dine with them the first evening in their new home. He was dressed in the uniform of a Union officer, and was greeted very warmly by Browning. His first inquiry was for Lulu, who was soon presented by her father.

"Do you know this gentleman, Lulu?" he asked.

She looked at him very earnestly, then at her father and Teenah.

"Teenah knows him," she replied, "but I do not! I think he looks something like darling mamma."

The stranger took her in his arms and kissed her, too much overcome to speak. It was her mamma's only brother—her uncle John, whom she had seen but once, and that more than two years before.

Teenah recognised him at once, as her countenance testified. He recollected her, too, and had a kind word for his sister's favorite.

Hunter entered the service with the first volunteers from his native State, and had been advanced in rank from Lieutenant to a Major. The accidental meeting of the brothers-in-law at Fernándina was a surprise and pleasure to both. For nearly a year they had heard nothing of one another, all communications ceasing at the commencement of hostilities. The tidings of Mrs. Browning's death had not reached her home in New Hampshire, although her last letter had prepared them for the event.

They remained in Fernandina two months; then when the weather grew warmer, too warm for health or comfort, Browning yielded to the importunity of his wife's friends and took Lulu and Teenah North.

The children were delighted with the rugged rocks, green fields, and blossoming orchards, and were soon content to remain amid the grand old mountains which they never were weary of gazing upon. They had seen nothing like them in their own summer land.

Teenah was more than contented. You had but to see her each morning dressing Lulu, gathering up their books in a pretty green satchel, then singing on her way to school, to know she was happy. She was truly happy, for she was drinking from the fount of

knowledge for which she had long been thirsting.

The children are still at school together, and
are making rapid progress. Lulu has not yet
learned to write plainly; but as often as her
father receives one of Teenah's well composed
and neatly written letters, he affirms, " She is a
genius, and shall be sent to Oberlin yet, where
she will be more fully prepared to become a
teacher to her own emancipated race." Should
this ever happen, we will tell our young readers about it in another little story.

LUCY LEE;

OR,

ALL THINGS FOR CHRIST.

LUCY'S RIDE WITH THE DOCTOR.

LUCY LEE.

CHAPTER I.

In a small cottage farm-house, up among the Green Mountains of Vermont, lived Lucy Lee. Though a little girl, she was the oldest of a whole group of brothers and sisters. There were Harry, Charley, Ruth, and Hetty, who was still in the cradle. Her parents, though quite intelligent people, were by no means rich. Like most of the farmers of New England with growing families, they were obliged to get their living by the "sweat of the brow," or, in other words, by constant, persevering toil.

Almost as soon as Lucy could walk she was

taught to be useful. She could dust chairs after her mother had been sweeping, rock the cradle while she made bread and cakes, and do a great many other things before she had learned to spell her own name. The neighbors thought her an uncommon womanly child, and held her up as an example to their own more thoughtless, or less dextrous little daughters. Her mother acknowledged her handiness, though often complaining of her want of life and vivacity. She said: "Although Lucy always performed her tasks well, and never did any mischief, somehow she wasn't *winsome* like most children. She wanted to see her *chirper*, and do things as if her mind was upon them, and not off in the clouds, or somewhere else, nobody knew where."

With four little ones younger than herself to be cared for, Lucy, at eight years old, was scarcely thought of as a child, with a child's yearnings for tenderness and affection, and with a child's need, too, of pastime and refreshment. She had never cared for play, after the common manner of childhood; crockery-houses and rag dolls were far more irksome to her than the little living things she was called upon to watch over continually. She loved her brothers and sisters dearly, yet there were times when their incessant clatter and cries seemed more than she could bear. They deafened her to her own thoughts, so she could not hear the voice of the spirit within, whose soft whispers were her solace in every grief and discouragement. Sometimes when **very** weary she would run away to the river-bank, and hide among the willows until she felt soothed and calmed. Then, in a tone that sounded like the gurgle of the waters or the warbling of birds, she often repeated the sweet hymns she learned at the Sabbath-school, or thought of the wonderful story of the Babe of Bethlehem, who was born in a manger and died upon the cross. Lucy knew that story in all its painful and affecting details, and sometimes told it to her little brothers, and bade them be gentle and good like the child Jesus. The hymn of the shepherds was the lullaby she loved most to sing while rocking her little sister's cradle, and Harry and Charley could sing with her:

"Cold on his cradle the dew-drops are shining;
  Lone lies his head with the beasts of the stall:
  Angels adore him, in slumbers reclining,
  Maker and Monarch and Saviour of all."

Lucy's home was in a wild spot, shut in on all sides by hills and mountains. Old " Ascutney" reared its bald head to the north, the rugged "Hawk" lay to the west, while peak after peak, whose names she did not know, stretched southward as far as the eye could reach.

Almost every child likes to gaze upon mountains, and watch the clouds and mists playing around their tops. Even Lucy's two little brothers loved to watch the giant white cloud-forms, to see whether they would rise up in the air or fall to the ground again, for their father had told them to look for fine weather when the white mist struggled upwards. But to Lucy the mountains were sublime, solemn mysteries. She never looked upon them without a feeling of longing and restlessness and pain. Sometimes they made her think of the great temples she read about in the Bible, with the incense smoking upon their altars, and thronged with white-robed ministers. Again they were only barriers, shutting out the narrow valley in which she lived from a sight of the great world. At such times she longed exceedingly to stand upon their tops and get a glimpse beyond. In one of these moods she asked so many questions, and manifested so much curiosity, that her father promised to take her some day to the summit of the highest, that she might see for herself, and be satisfied.

Lucy had never been any further from the cottage than the parish church, which lay up the valley a little more than two miles away, and her father's promise made her heart as light as a bird's. She thought of it days, and dreamed about it nights, until, one fine, clear, autumn morning, she saw the grey pony harnessed

17

to the old yellow wagon, and heard her father call her to put on her things quickly for a ride. She was ready in a few minutes, and climbing joyfully over the pile of bags which Mr. Lee was going to drop at the grist-mill on the way. It was Lucy's first ride for pleasure.

Pretty soon after leaving the village, the narrow road began to wind upwards, and kept winding higher and higher, until Lucy began to think they must be nearing the clouds. The grey pony went forward steadily and patiently until they gained the summit, and then his master dropped the lines, and bade him rest.

Lucy was wholly unprepared for the extent and grandeur of the prospect which burst upon her; but not a single exclamation fell from her lips as her father pointed out by the white steeples town after town, and then showed her in the distance Monadnock and Holyoke and Tom, whose tops seemed resting on the skies. The Connecticut wound like a silver ribbon through its beautiful green valley, until away.

to the south it looked only like a little thread of sunshine. They lingered some time before the horse's head was turned homeward, for Mr. Lee from his boyhood had loved the moun- tain-tops, and for many years had not beheld them in their autumnal splendor before.

Lucy wept herself to sleep that night with- out knowing whether for joy or sorrow. Her father said she had got tired and was nervous; her mother that she had better have stayed at home and tended the baby, as her head was too full of notions before.

Mrs. Lee was a plain practical woman, and knew very little about the world of imagi- nation. Her child might "see visions and dream dreams," but certainly she did not in- herit the inclination from her mother, whose organ of ideality had never grown to visible size. God's mountains were simply moun- tains to her, built up of dark rocks, and covered with dwarf cedars and scraggy pines. Why her husband should talk so foolishly about them to the children, she could not well understand.

CHAPTER II.

Lucy had never been to school. There was no school nearer than the village, and that was a long way for a little girl to walk, especially without company. When Harry was four years old, they commenced a term together; but in less than a week the little fellow gave out, then school was given up altogether. Mr. Lee taught Lucy some things himself when he had time, and she repeated his lessons to the younger children. She was an apt scholar, and with what help she could get by asking questions made more rapid proficiency than some children with the best of instruction. With time and books, she would have kept pace with any child of her own age; but between the washing of dishes, dusting, and tending baby, Lucy had seldom an hour to herself, though she lived in a world of her own, into which no one had ever entered. It was a world of thoughts and feelings; a strange, perplexing world for so young a child. She could never bring her mind to speak of it, not even when chided by her mother, as she often was, for stupidity or absent-mindedness. A nature like hers, so keenly alive to every breeze that blows upon it, is never too young to feel and know if it is misunderstood or misinterpreted.

But pleasanter days were dawning for Lucy. At another farm-house, about half a mile from theirs, a stranger lady was about to open a school, and Lucy, Harry, and Charley were going. Little Ruth was too small, and baby was not out of the standing-stool. The lady had been for some years a teacher at the West, and had come to spend a season with her sister among the mountains of Vermont. Finding many children in the neighborhood, her sister's among the number, too young to walk to the village school, she offered to instruct them through the winter, and her offer was hailed with great joy by their parents.

As soon as Thanksgiving was over, the school commenced. About a dozen little ones, between the ages of four and ten, gathered daily around dear Miss Willis, one of the kindest, best teachers who ever undertook to guide simple feet in the paths of knowledge. There was no ruggedness nor difficulty which her gentle patience did not soon render plain and pleasant. She taught them a great many things not found in their books; told them pleasant stories to illustrate their lessons and make them remember them, and strove in every way to do them good and make them happy. Every young heart opened unconsciously to the new teacher, showing her what pleasures and hopes and griefs had already entered those little throbbing life-chambers; and for each and all she had some kind word of encouraging sympathy.

Though devoted to her pupils alike, none of them interested Miss Willis like Lucy Lee, the modest, motherly child, to whom all the younger ones in school looked for care and direction. She had never met a child of more marked intellectual character, or one who manifested as plainly the tastes and temperament of genius. What could she do for such a shrinking sensitive nature, whose powers as yet were only like the feeble wings of an unfledged bird calling for brooding tenderness and cherishing love to make them grow strong, and aid them to unfold rightly? Miss Willis knew well how many such natures, chilled by adverse circumstances, never expand to full size; which, for ever fluttering, can never mount up into the higher atmosphere of their kindred.

Lucy knew nothing of what was so often in her teacher's mind. She knew only that she never laughed at her strange questionings, or chided her for not thinking and talking about such things as other children did. So, as she became better acquainted, her heart opened unconsciously, and revealed to her new friend depths of thought and feeling which none had discovered before. Often at recess, while string-ing a boy's kite, or mending a ball, or showing some little girl **how to cut** paper-roses, would Miss **Willis** whisper a quaint story to Lucy **Lee, or repeat** some **old** legend, **which she** knew would recreate the young student more than all the amusements which her compa-nions loved.

Miss Willis's stories **were very** different from the nursery tales, "Old Mother Hubbard," "London Bridge," or "Jack's Bean," the only stories Lucy had ever heard, except her favor-ite Bible stories. She listened with rapt atten-tion to the fanciful tales of "Undine" and of "Echo," or of the beautiful sisters of "Hyas," who wept themselves to stars for the loss of their brother. The stories of "Iduna and her Apples" and of "Bifrost," **the** "Rainbow Bridge," which nearly every child reads about now, were new to her and charmed her exceed-ingly. They were something like the myths of her own busy imagination.

Spelling, writing, grammar, geography, or arithmetic, never wearied the little ones at Miss Willis's school, though they studied hard, and made rapid proficiency ; for intellectual pastime was rightly blended with intellectual labor. Teaching is one of the fine arts, for which few are divinely gifted, though a host of men and women enter upon it as unfitly as the mechanic artisan, who, with a dollar-and-cent eye. alone, should set up for a Claude Lorraine. More delicate even than his should be the teacher's *touches*, who draws on a young child's heart lines for immortality. Miss Willis was eminently endowed by nature for her favorite pursuit. She had not only a faculty to impart knowledge, but the principle to leave no false impression on the minds of her tender learners. What each budding nature required for a vigorous unfolding was her most earnest study, while her daily prayer arose for heavenly counsel and direction.

18

CHAPTER III.

THE winter among the mountains passed delightfully with the little ones who attended the farm-house school. Lucy, who had never used a pen before, was soon able to write a plain, pretty hand, and could analyse and parse a sentence better than many an older grammarian. Harry could travel anywhere on the map of the United States with his eyes shut, and tell the largest cities, the longest rivers, and the highest mountains on the globe; and he could numerate as many figures besides as the black-board would hold. The little things who commenced at A B C were soon reading about " *Feeding the Old Hen*," or doing some other more wonderful feat, to the astonishment of their parents, who thought them all prodigies.

No day was stormy enough to keep them home peaceably. If the snow fell, and the cold winds blew it up in heaps ever so high, the great oxen could break through the drifts and draw them on the wide sled safely to the school-room door. The colder the day, the warmer they knew would be their teacher's greeting, and the better their chances for a pleasant story at recess.

One cold, blustering January morning, the young Lees carried an extra basket with them to school. It was filled with corn popped white as the Vermont snow-flakes. Miss Willis was very fond of it, and the basket was for her. She smiled as she took it, and told them her next story should be an Indian Corn Legend.

That very noon it was snowing and blowing, so they could not play out of the house, and the children reminded the teacher of her promise. She went and brought a portfolio, and from a number of papers selected the following, which she read:

Come around me, little children,
　　This stormy winter morn,
And I will tell you a story
　　About the Indian Corn—
Which grew first up in heaven
　　(The story-tellers say),
Till the Master of all Spirits
　　Spoke thus to it one day:

"**Go** down to the earth, Mondamin!
　　My children there lack food!
Grow tall and strong in the valleys,
　　And do the Redmen good.
They shall not hurt nor waste you,
　　But foster you with care;
And plant in the spring-time only
　　Sufficient for one year."

Then dropped the good Mondamin,
　　Like dew, from heaven to earth:
And the Redmen danced new dances
　　In honor of his worth.
They praised his golden tresses,
　　And his form so tall and slim,
Till Mondamin loved the Redmen,
　　And the Redmen all loved him.

But one year the great Miamies
   Forgot the Master's rule,
And left the stranger standing,
   When all their sacks were full,
Within the open cornfield,
   Where the idlers went each morn
To throw at one another
   The broken ears of corn.

The Master of Life beheld them!
   And when his children went
To their winter hunt in the forests
   Where deer abounded, He sent
Aside the point of each arrow,
   And led in a weary plight
The empty-handed hunters
   Back to their camp at night.

An old man spake one morning,
   And said: "I am weak, my son!
For meat or broth I am fainting!"
   His son replied: "Not one
Of the oldest of our hunters
   Can kill with bow or spear!
The Redman's God must be angry,
   For the forests are full of deer."

Next morn that same young hunter
  Went forth again, to try
To kill some game for his father,
  Who was old and ready to die.
All day he wandered vainly
  'Mid herds he could not kill,
Till he lost his way in the forest,
  And came to a little rill

With a wigwam close beside it.
  Quoth he: "I will rest to-night
Until morning lift the curtain
  Of the Eastern House of Light;
For I have no meat for my father!"
  As his steps to the lodge drew nigher,
He saw an old man sitting
  With his back turned towards the fire.

"Grandfather, your child is weary!"
  The youthful hunter said.
"All day he has roved in the forest—
  All day he has tasted no bread!
The little ones of his nation
  And the aged cry for food,
But dull is the aim of the hunter,
  While the deer run wild in the wood."

" My son," said the old man, groaning,
　"There is food in the kettle, you'll find:
Go satisfy your hunger,
　And then I will speak my mind."
When the repast was over,
　He opened his mouth, and said:
"O! cruel and vain Miamies,
　Whom I so long have fed !

By them was my back-bone broken !
　By them was I bruised and torn,
And none said: ''Tis poor Mondamin,
　The Spirit of the Corn!'
But my cry went up to heaven ;
　And the good Great Father said:
'I will give to that nation famine
　Till the living eat their dead!'"

The hunter rose next morning
　And went back to his clan,
Where every word he repeated
　Of that broken-backed old man.
And never since then at harvest
　Has an Indian treated with scorn
The body of Mondamin,
　The Spirit of the Corn.

The children were delighted with the "Corn Legend," and asked so many questions about the Indians, and whether they really believed such queer things, that Miss Willis hardly knew how to answer them. She said many of the Indian tribes believed the corn a sacred grain, and that great famine would follow its waste or abuse; which was in a measure true, as they depended upon it more than upon anything else for their winter food. Every tribe had some wonderful tradition respecting its origin, similar to the one she had just read to them. They would altogether make a large book. The Indians had great respect and veneration for their old traditions, she told them, and would be far less likely to destroy the cornfields of their enemies, or waste their own grain, if taught it was a spirit-gift, and under the special protection of the "Master of Life."

Then she talked with them a long time about the customs of the Redmen, some of which are very beautiful, and others dreadfully savage. Miss Willis had visited a number of tribes in their own homes, and was acquainted with their habits as well as with their traditionary stories.

When the clock struck one, the children could scarcely believe an hour had passed so quickly, and that the intermission was over. Lucy asked permission to copy the Corn Legend some time, and was promised that and other legends besides. Then the scholars went to their seats, and strove by their diligence and good behavior to show that they were not ungrateful for their teacher's love and kindness.

19

CHAPTER IV.

Not one of Miss Willis's scholars was glad to feel the warm breath of spring among their native hills; for with the spring they would lose their beloved teacher. · The winter, though a very cold and stormy one, had seemed too short to them all. Lucy grieved more than the others in prospect of their loss, and often asked herself what she could do when school was over. She had learned a great deal in one winter—among other things, how much there is to be learned—which she had never known about before Miss Willis came. Who would direct her how to do, and what to do first, when she was gone away? Her mother could not; she had her hands full of labor, and did not care much any way for the things Lucy fancied most. Her father, who understood her nature and disposition better, was always at work providing for the daily bread of his little flock, and had very little time to question or instruct. If he couldn't give them much education, he reasoned, they must manage to live without it as he had done; but food to eat and clothes to wear they must have or die. How many such parents there are in the world, with strength and energies all exhausted in procuring the common, every-day necessities of life, who have neither time to attend to the wants of the immortal nature nor means to satisfy its cravings! Little do children, whose paths are surrounded with luxuries, and who neglect to improve the privileges lavished upon them, think how many young hearts would be made rich with only a small share of what they possess! The very books you so carelessly destroy, my little friends, would have made Lucy Lee happy for a long time; and the lessons they contain would have added to her life-long store of wisdom.

In Mr. Lee's house were only a Bible and a

psalm-book, a volume of Watts's lyric poems, and a copy of Shakspeare, purchased when he was a young man, and made his first and only visit to New York. All of these Lucy had read since she could spell out the first words, and they had tinged with a warmer glow her naturally poetic nature. Her father often said, if a person had a Bible for Sunday, and a Shakspeare for winter evenings, he had always reading enough.

When the children wanted school-books, they saved their nuts and sent them to market with part of the winter apples, and the new spelling-books, Testament, grammar, geography, and arithmetic, seemed to them more than compensation for their loss. Their father had a slate, which was newly framed for them, and so the children were fitted for school. Their mother put *thumb-marks* into the new books for their better preservation, for things procured with difficulty and self-denial are apt to be cared for more than those which follow the mere asking.

After Lucy had learned to write, Miss Willis presented her with a neat blank book, in which she might copy anything that pleased her. Before spring she had written within it several very pretty poems, and two or three wild Indian legends, something like the one in the last chapter. One of them was about a little boy who was changed to a robin redbreast on account of fasting too long. The other was a story of a youth who wandered away to the spirit-land to find the soul of his dead sister. He found her and brought her home in a gourd. Lucy often read over these fanciful stories to herself, and sometimes to her father and mother. Mr. Lee said they were real Indian-like, and he wished Miss Willis had more such; but his wife thought there wasn't a bit of sense to them, and wondered how so good a teacher could be putting such nonsense into children's heads.

The last day of school came soon. It was the first of April, a pleasant, sunshiny day, but none of the little ones felt like *April fool-*

ing as usual. Lucy shed many tears by the
way that morning, and her eyes were red when
she entered the school-room. Miss Willis felt
very sad as she went through the exercises for
the last time, not knowing whether she would
ever meet the dear children again in the world.
After the lessons were over, she talked to them
kindly and tenderly; bade them be good children, and try to grow up good men and
women. She counselled them earnestly to
honor their parents; to love one another; and
above all, to love and fear God, their kind,
heavenly parent. She was going far from
them, and hoped never to hear a bad report of
any one of them. Then she knelt down, and
prayed that they might all be watched over
and protected, wherever their young feet might
wander on the uncertain journey of life, and
be gathered together again in the Saviour's
fold at the end of the way.

After giving to each some little token of remembrance, the pleasant school at the farm-
house was dismissed. When they had gather-

ed up their books, the children went one by
one for a last kiss, then ran home quickly to
show their respective gifts.

All but Lucy. She remained a little longer
with Miss Willis, who wished to say some
things to her, which she could not say so well
in presence of the whole school. As soon as
the little ones were all gone, she sat down on
the bench beside her, and took her hand kindly in her own. She was too much affected by
the child's half-smothered grief to speak at
first; but when she did, her voice was clear
and sweet as usual.

"I am very sorry to leave you," she said;
" but such things have to be, all through life.
I have been much interested in you, Lucy, and
shall be so still when we are separated. Con-
tinue to improve as you have done, my child."

" But I shall have no one to help me when
you are gone," interrupted Lucy, with sobs. " I
am afraid I shall never go to school again, or
learn anything more."

" You mustn't get discouraged, my dear.

You are a little girl yet, and have many years to learn in. I have marked some lessons for you to study by yourself in the history I gave you this afternoon, and have written in a letter, which you will find inside, some things I wish you to think about. You can write to me whenever you find any difficulty which you cannot overcome, and I shall always feel pleased to give you my opinion. I think, with a little practice, you will find it very easy to express your thoughts on paper. Have you ever tried, Lucy ? "

" I have only written down the things you gave me in my book."

" I will send you some more, Lucy; and you shall write how they please you. I have another little present for you in my desk."

Miss Willis went and brought a small portfolio filled with paper and envelopes. "It is not a new one," she said ; "I have used it for many years, but am sure you will not like it the less on that account. You will find a card of pens and some pencils in one part; so you will have everything handy when you wish to write. Now, my dear, you must promise me to do your best, and some day, perhaps, you will come West and be a teacher; or I should not be surprised if you should write books for children to read. You can do almost anything you try, I know, Lucy. You recollect those beautiful lines you copied, don't you?

> " ' Lives of great men all remind us
>   We may make our lives sublime ;
> And departing, leave behind us
>   Footsteps on the sands of Time :
> Footsteps that perhaps another,
>   Sailing o'er life's stormy main,
> Some forlorn and shipwrecked brother,
>   Seeing, may take heart again! ' "

Miss Willis never spoke to Lucy Lee as to most other children of her age; for her thoughts were not like those of ordinary children. When she had done talking to her, Lucy strove in vain for words to thank her for all her kindness. Miss Willis read in her grate-

20

ful looks and tearful eyes the expression she could not utter, and with a last silent kiss they parted.

CHAPTER V.

School was over, and Miss Willis gone.
There were some dreary days among the
mountains that spring, days when winter
seemed about to return with all its stormy fol-
lowers. Lucy found very little opportunity to
study, for they kept but one fire, and the children were noisier, and more impatient of restraint, for the few days of sunshine they had
enjoyed. She had a little room up-stairs under
the cottage eaves, where she slept and kept her
few treasures. One rainy day her father made
her a small pine table, with a drawer in it for
her books and portfolio, that she might keep
them out of the way of the children. She
was more pleased with the simple arrangement
than many girls I have known with very rich-
ly furnished apartments. But it was too cold

for her to sit there now, and, besides, her mother had a good deal of knitting and sewing for her when the house-work was done. So she worked all day busy as a bee, thinking how pleasant it would be when the long warm days came, and she could find a little time for the lessons Miss Willis had marked out for her.

After the younger children were put to bed, Lucy sometimes went for her history, and asked her father to read aloud, while her mother sewed, and she knit upon his long stockings. This was very pleasant; and Lucy, after listening to his reading, often went to bed to dream of Christopher Columbus and his wanderings from kingdom to kingdom to find some one able and willing to help him go and make discoveries. One night she dreamed of going herself to Queen Isabella, and begging she would send the old man to look up the beautiful new world beyond the ocean. The Queen promised her, and Lucy awoke bewildered with joy, to hear the rain pattering on the roof of the little farm-house among the mountains.

There was a wide difference betwixt her low, dark chamber, and the great shining palace of royalty through which she had been wandering in a dream. She was very glad, however, to think that Columbus had found his new world, and that, safe in her little table drawer, she had more than three hundred years of its history.

But the evenings soon grew too short, and her father too weary after a hard day's work, to read any more. Lucy was very sorry, but it could not be helped.

The mountain-tops lost their white caps of snow, and there was less rain and more days of sunshine. The children heard a bluebird singing one morning in the orchard, and it made their pulses beat quicker, as the first bird-song always does after a long winter of ice and snow. The robins came soon after, and chirped around the door and picked up the crumbs. One of them began a nest in the old lilac-bush, where there had been a nest every year since the children could remember.

Lucy told her brothers what the Indians thought the reason the redbreast was tamer than other birds, and why it always loved to be around human habitations. They were much interested, and wished her to read the whole story to them. So she went for her portfolio, and sat down on the door-stone, in the sun, and read the " Legend of the Redbreast," just as dear Miss Willis had given it to her. As some of my young readers may like to know what it was, I will write it down here for them to read too:

LEGEND OF THE REDBREAST.

Many marvellous stories
  Do the fanciful Redmen tell,
When the lodge-fires burn at evening,
  And the wintry storms compel
From the hunt of the bear and the bison:
  There is one I remember well.

I heard it not in the wigwam
  In the midst of a dusky ring,
But away in the Northern forest
  On a pleasant morn in spring,

With robins singing around me,
   And blossoms awakening.

There was once a Chippewa hunter
   From youth bred up to the chase,
Who at length grew over-ambitious;
   And shadows fell dark on his face
As he marked how the men of the war-trail
   Sat next to the chiefs in place.

Moody he went in the morning
   To the forest with his spear;
Moody he came at evening
   And laid at his door the deer,
Till Wâsayâh, "Light of the Wigwam."
   Wept many a sorrowful tear.

A change had come over her hunter;
   She whispered the tale to none,
But folded her heart-strings closer
   And fonder around her son,
The last of Wâsayâh's children,
   Her delicate Wanbegoon.*

The boy was a marvel of beauty;
   But for boyhood too tender and fair.
His cheek was soft as a maiden's,
   As silken and glossy his hair;

* "Little Blossom."—*Chippewa.*

Not a child in the Chippewa country
  Had ever so gentle an air.

There was light in the eye of the hunter,
  And joy in his spirit again,
As he marked how his son grew in stature!
  And he taught him the lore of his clan,
And called him Ne-gitch-e-dan-een,
  "His brave little Warrior-man."

The suns rolled round in the heavens;
  The red boy was twelve years old,
Still timid and tender as ever,
  Though so often his father had told
Him he never should grow up a hunter,
  But a warrior bloody and bold.

The fasting days were approaching;
  Those days of highest esteem,
When the red youth seeth in vision
  A destiny supreme,
And the paths of his life are appointed
  By the spirit of his dream.

Then the hunter went forth one morning,
  And built, with an air of pride,
A lodge of the fragrant birches
  That grew by the river's side;

While Wâsayâh, weeping, was weaving
   The mat her love would provide.

That evening the voice of the father
   Exhorted the lad to be strong;
To quail not, nor faint like a woman;
   But the days of his fast to prolong
Till the voice of a powerful spirit
   Should teach him the warrior's song.

Poor Ningwis, the gentle and yielding,
   Gave promise his wish to fulfil;
He watched the form of his father,
   Till it vanished over the hill;
Then lay down on his mat of green rushes,
   With a meek and obedient will.

But that summer night was so lonely!
   The sounds he had loved to hear
When sitting beside the wigwam
   Grew terrible in his ear;
The night-bird's song in the forest,
   And the wolf's howl, made him fear.

The whippoorwill's cry was mournful,
   The katydid's made him weep;
But he called on the guardian spirits
   That over the universe keep

Soft watches of love for the lonely!
  Then quietly fell asleep.

Eight days, with no word of complaining,
  The youth kept his torturing fast;
Poor Wâsayâh wept in her wigwam,
  Loathing her own repast,
While Ningwis grew fainter and weaker;
  But he spake to his father at last:

"My dreams are not good, O my father!
  The spirit that cometh to me
Shows not the paths of the warriors;
  And this fasting is agony.
But give me a morsel this morning,
  And I'll try it again for thee."

"Not yet, not yet!" said the hunter,
  "Or all will be lost that is won!
Have courage a little longer,
  And the spirits will come, my son!
The *great* ones who lead on the war-trail—
  Your fasting will then be done!"

He covered his face with his blanket,
  The depth of his anguish to hide.
Eleven days he fasted and famished,
  When his sire stood again by his side,

"Food! food!" was all he could utter.
  More gently his father replied:

"To-morrow I'll come with it early,
  While the light of the dawning is dim,
'Tis the last dark night of your weakness,
  Then cometh the victory-hymn!"
Alas! for the morning and evening
  Were getting alike to him!

A mist hung over his eyelids;
  His strength had forsaken him quite;
And he lay like one passively dying
  All the lone, long, sorrowful night;
But a spirit came with the daybreak
  And brought to the dark one light.

And with food to the lodge next morning
  The hunter impatiently sped;
And lo! there poor Ningwis was sitting
  Erect on his rush-woven bed,
Grey wings grown out of his shoulders,
  And his breast all feathered and red.

"My son! my son! do not leave me,"
  In anguish the father conjured!
"Live in peace in the home of the hunter!"
  The lad answered never a word,

But flew to the top of the wigwam
  In the shape of a beautiful bird.

He sang as he went: "My change should not grieve you,
I am happier now, and I never will leave you!
I can give you sweet songs, for the bird is my brother,
The bird that watched over my slumbers when young,
And Ningwis each morning will sing to his mother
As he sits on the bough where his cradle was hung.
He can pick the red berries high-up on the tree,
And sing to the children, 'Pee-chee! O-pee-chee.'
He will faint not from weakness, nor groan under care:
With his bed on the tree-top, his path in the air,
The meadows and mountains will furnish him food."
Thus ending his song, he flew off to the wood.

    Such is the singular story
      The fanciful Redmen tell,
    When asked why O-pee-chee, the redbreast,
      Loveth men's haunts so well.
    And the tawny children hear it
      By the winter lodge-fire's blaze,
    And tell it o'er on the prairies
      In the pleasant strawberry days.

Every Indian youth, arriving at a certain
age, retires to some lonely spot to fast for his

guardian spirit. Sometimes he goes to the top of a high hill or mountain, sometimes to the forest, or to some lonely island in the waters, where he waits for the coming of his life-guide. Whatever object appears to him there becomes sacred through all the years to come. To such guardian spirits, the poor, superstitious Redmen direct their prayers for help in every time of need, as well as their war-songs and death-songs.

Lucy and her brothers talked a long time about poor Ningwis and his sad fate. Lucy thought perhaps the ambition of the hunter was told as a warning for people to be contented with their own lot. She did not know, for, like all Indian stories, it was very strange and wild. Harry and Charley didn't believe a word about it, any way; and yet they said they should never kill a robin if they could help it, nor ever see one again without thinking of Ningwis and his cruel father.

CHAPTER VI.

ONE bright morning, about the first of May, after the breakfast things were washed and put away, Lucy's mother told her to take the broom and sweep the chambers. She went first to the one occupied by her brothers. It was a large back room, and as bare of furniture as bare could be. A low bedstead stood in one corner, with a blue, home-made coverlet spread over it; the figures upon it looking so much like rough-shelled butternuts, the little fellows used to wake up and count them in the morning. The naked rafters were hung with last year's herbs: May-weed, boneset, tansy, elder-flowers, and a great variety of mints, all dried and blackened with age. A long meal-chest, divided into several compartments for the various kinds of meal and flour, stood before one window, with a bread-trough inverted on the cover; for this was all the store-room the cottage contained. A spinning-wheel, reel, and *swifts*, or *winders*, occupied another corner; and this, with a broken chair or two, is a correct inventory of articles in the boys' chamber. Even to Lucy, who had never, except in dreams, seen a fine house, the room looked dark and mean; and she made haste to throw up the windows and let in the bird-songs and sweet spring breezes. Then the bed was made neatly, and the room brushed and dusted as carefully as though it had been a palace chamber.

Afterwards she went to her own apartment, which was smaller and more suggestive of comfort. Instead of bare rafters, the walls were coarsely plastered and whitewashed; and the one window was curtained with a width of flowered wall-paper, left when the best room was papered below. The bed was as low and plainly dressed as her brothers'; but near it stood the little pine table which held her treasures, and she forgot the nakedness of the floor, and the absence of decoration, in the thought of these gifts of her beloved teacher.

The window was wide open, and a bough of the old sugar-maple-tree that shaded the house reached almost to the casement, red with blossoms, and rich with perfume. Honey-bees were humming around it and sipping its sweets. A bluebird was carrying threads and wisps of straw through a hole which a red-headed woodpecker had tapped in its hollow trunk, while an old robin put the finishing touches to a nest she had been busily working upon for a number of days.

Lucy forgot her work for once, and sat down beside the window to look and listen. The very air seemed to be full of rejoicing that bright spring morning. A little way off, in the hill-pasture, she could hear the voices of the young lambs, and see their merry gambols among the rocks. Nothing is pleasanter in spring-time than to watch the playful lambs.

"I wonder if I couldn't write something

about this beautiful morning!" Lucy exclaimed at last. "I never tried to compose anything myself, but Miss Willis thought it would
be easy for me with practice. I mean to try
now."

She did not open the drawer for her nice
paper and pens. She had a little bit of a
wooden pencil in her pocket, and a torn leaf
of an old account-book figured all over on one
side. These were good enough, she thought,
for her first scribbling; so she wrote "Spring"
on the top of the paper, as almost every child
does for the first composition, then fell into a
deep study.

Very soon her fingers began to play; a line
or two were written; then there was another
stop and study. So she sat wholly absorbed
in her new exercise an hour or more. Sometimes her lips moved, sometimes her fingers,
until at last she started up and said: "I have
done it! Yes! I have done it."

She dropped her pencil, forgot her broom
and everything else in the first joy of author-

ship. "I thought it would come to me some time," she mused; "for when I sleep I often repeat verses that are not in any book I ever saw. When I wake up, they ring in my ears a long time, though I could never put them together again so they would sound right. I am so glad I have done this!"

And Lucy looked glad as she ran down the rough uncarpeted stairs, and stood with her torn leaf in her hand in the presence of her mother.

"Mother, won't you listen?" she said, going near and taking hold of her dress. "I have said something myself about this pleasant spring morning, and want you to hear it."

"*Said something yourself!*" exclaimed her mother, not quite comprehending Lucy's meaning. "Why, you've got something written there, haven't you?"

"Yes! but then I said it to myself first, you know. I didn't write it out of any book, and no one told it to me either."

"Well, well, then, make haste with your

nonsense, or else the baby will wake up before the work is done."

Lucy commenced, and read in a trembling voice the two following verses upon "*Spring:*"

> The winter is past, the spring has returned,
>   And all things look lively and gay,
> The robins and bluebirds together have come,
>   And the country resounds with their lay.
>
> The lambs on the sunny south hill-side are seen
>   Frisking and frolicking,
> And the trees in the orchard begin to look green,
>   In the smiles of the beautiful spring.

With a half-smile on her lips, Mrs. Lee listened to her daughter's first composition. When it was finished, she 'laughed aloud. Lucy looked up for some word of approbation, but her mother only said: "What sort of a line do you call that, Frisking 'and frolicking?' It is a dreadful short one beside the others, and hasn't much sense in it either."

"I know, mother! The line didn't suit me

but then I had to have some word at the end
of it to sound like spring, and couldn't think
of anything better."

" That's always the way with folks that make
such sort of nonsense. Don't you go to trying
to make verses, Lucy, for nobody was ever
known to be good for anything else who did.
I dare say the chambers won't be half swept,
now you've been fooling."

"The boys' is well done, mother; mine
isn't," Lucy answered truthfully.

" I thought as much.   Go now, and don't
let me hear any more about your ' frisking and
frolicking.' "

Never did a child fall quicker from a height
of happiness than did Lucy Lee. She had
looked for some little word of commendation
or encouragement, and had received only ridi-
cule instead, which was very mortifying to a
nature like hers. Tears filled her eyes, but
pride forbade their falling until she had reached
her own chamber and buttoned fast the door.
Then she wept and sobbed as though her

young heart were breaking. The brightness
of that May morning no longer shone in Lucy's
heart. The music and beauty of the outer
world were alike forgotten.

After the first outburst of disappointed feeling, she wiped her eyes, tore the unfortunate
paper in two, and was about to rend it in frag-
ments when another thought seemed to take
possession of her mind. What it was she
never told, but the pieces of her composition
were folded together carefully and placed in
a little pasteboard box in her drawer, wet with
her tears. The tumbled bed was then laid together, and the neglected broom completed the
morning's work.

By the time it was done, she was called to
get the potatoes for dinner, which she did with
a spirit from which all the life and sparkle had
fled. Not even her father's proposition that
she should go with the boys for artichokes that
afternoon could restore her joyousness, though
she felt very glad to go out for awhile in the
cheerful sunshine.

For some days Lucy went about the house very quietly and soberly. Her father noticed it, and thought she was wishing to go to school again, she had been so lively and cheerful while that lasted. Her mother said there was no use saying a word to her about walking to the village; it was too far, and besides she could not spare her.

CHAPTER VII.

ONE rainy afternoon, about a week after
Lucy's attempt at verse-making, her father
came home from the village with a pleased,
happy look. "What do you think I've got
for *Miss Lucy Lee?*" he asked, as she was
making haste to set the supper-table. "Something, I hope, which will bring sunshine to her
sorry-looking face."

He took a letter from his pocket, with a
white envelope, sealed neatly with red wax,
and held it up before the eyes of the astonished
group, who were scarcely able to believe that
Lucy had got a letter directed to herself.

"'Tis from Miss Willis, I'll bet a cent!"
exclaimed Harry, as delighted as Lucy at the
very thought.

"Oh! I hope so," said Charley, hopping

about in high glee. "I do want to see Miss Willis."

"'Tis from *her*," said Lucy, "for I know her handwriting; and then here is "A. W." on the wax. Her name is Abby."

"Well, now," said her father pleasantly, "open it, and let's see what's inside."

"I want to read it to myself first," was Lucy's reply; and as soon as the last thing was on the supper-table, she ran away to her own chamber to enjoy the precious missive, every nerve of her frame trembling with delight. She broke the seal and read it from beginning to end; then commenced and read it again with eyes full of tears. How like her beloved teacher that letter was, in every word and line; full of love and anxious care still for the little ones she had guided so tenderly for a few months, and left, never to meet them again, perchance, in the uncertain journey of life!

The account of her journey interested Lucy very much, and she was sure it would interest her father and mother, and the children too. So she took it down and read it all to them. Then there was one of Longfellow's sweetest poems, which Miss Willis had cut from a paper for her, and sent with the request that she would write her just how she liked it. Mr. and Mrs. Lee wished to hear the poem, and Lucy read:

"The shades of night were falling fast,
When, through an Alpine village, passed
A youth, who bore, 'mid snow and ice,
A banner with the strange device—
　　　　　Excelsior!

His brow was sad; his eyes beneath
Flashed like a falchion from its sheath;
And like a silver clarion rung
The accents of that unknown tongue—
　　　　　Excelsior!

In happy homes, he saw the light
Of household fires gleam warm and bright;
Above, the spectral glaciers shone,
And from his lips escaped a groan—
　　　　　Excelsior!

23

'Try not the pass!' the old man said,
'Dark lowers the tempest overhead;
The roaring torrent is deep and wide!'
And loud that clarion voice replied—
　　　　　　Excelsior!

'Beware the pine-tree's withered branch!
Beware the awful avalanche!'
This was the peasant's last good night;
A voice replied, far up the height—
　　　　　　Excelsior!

At break of day, as heavenward
The pious monks of St. Bernard
Uttered the oft-repeated prayer,
A voice cried through the startled air—
　　　　　　Excelsior!

A traveller, by the faithful hound,
Half-buried in the snow was found,
Still grasping in his hand of ice
That banner with the strange device—
　　　　　　Excelsior!

There in the twilight, cold and grey,
Lifeless, but beautiful, he lay;

And from the sky serene, and far,
A voice fell, like a falling star—
                          Excelsior!"

Her father and mother listened attentively and silently until Lucy had finished the beautiful poem, and asked how they liked it. **Mr.** Lee brushed a tear from his eye as he said: "The story is very prettily told, but the **poor** youth had better have given **heed to** the words of the old man, who knew all the paths and passes better than he."

Her mother said: "That sort of folks always come to some bad end. There was no use in warning them, for, if they got out of one trouble alive, they'd be sure to get into another."

Lucy's eyes were bright with enthusiasm as she replied: "I don't think he came to a *bad end*, mother! Excelsior means *higher;* and the boy sang it all the way long until he stood upon the mountain-top, though it must have been hard for him sometimes. Then, when he saw nothing but the heavens and the stars above him, he wanted to go up and finish his song. I think it is beautiful where the voice fell back from the sky like a falling star."

Her father gazed with astonishment on Lucy's face as she spoke. He had never seen her so earnest in the expression of an opinion before; but he shook his head and said there might be such a thing as carrying a *will* too far. Harry said he liked the fellow's spunk. He knew before that *Excelsior* meant *higher*, for Miss Willis had told them so, and that it was the motto of the State of New York. He didn't believe his father could ask Miss Willis a single thing she didn't know.

Lucy was happy again that night as she lay upon her pillow, thinking of her letter, and all the kind, pleasant words it contained. The shadow that had rested on her young spirit was suddenly lifted. The perseverance of the Alpine youth amid chilling discouragements seemed sent to inspire her with new courage and hope. Lucy was not a Christian; therefore she could not see the light which the young Christian sees in all times of darkness. Though from early childhood she had known well the story of the Cross, and had wept over it again and again, she had never, like Bunyan's pious pilgrim, laid her burdens at its foot. Few children had read the Bible as much as she, or understood as well its heavenly counsels; but, like many others, she loved it better for its stirring stories than for the precepts which would make her wise unto salvation.

CHAPTER VIII.

THE next morning was a morning of spring brightness. The grass looked greener and the flowers brighter for the rain. Lucy thought she would like a run in the fields, but the baby was not well, and she felt it would be useless as well as wrong to ask to go before the work was done. When the sun got up higher, however, Mrs. Lee said she believed the warm out-of-door air would do little Hetty good, and if Lucy would draw her out in the wagon, she would finish the morning chores.

It was a pleasant proposition to Lucy, the more so because quite unexpected; and she ran quickly for her sun-bonnet and cape. The baby was warmly wrapped, and began to spring and jump at sight of the little wagon; and as she was drawn gently through the back gate into the orchard, it would have been difficult to say which of the sisters wore the brighter face.

Lucy knew where **there** was a warm sunny **south bank, and directed** her steps thither, only stopping now and then to pull a dandelion **or a** daisy for little Hetty. When they gained their resting-place, the child's lap was full of shining blossoms, which she played with, crowed over, and pulled in pieces with the greatest glee, while Lucy sat down beside her on the warm hillside, looking away to the grand old moun- **tains one** minute, and down upon the sweet **blue** violets at her feet the next. The apple orchard was just budding into blossom, and the **birds poured** forth their joy in full notes of thanksgiving.

"Happy little singers!" Lucy exclaimed. "How I wish I could help you!" Before she was aware, her lips were moving, and her thoughts expressing themselves in simple rhyme. The mortification that followed her first attempt was quite forgotten as she pen- cilled the following lines:

The violets are springing
   Upon the hillsides now,
And the little birds are singing
   On every budding bough ;
To them it is a pleasure
   To warble all day long,
And oh ! if I had leisure,
   I'd try to sing a song.

I'd sing about the mountains
   That stand up to the skies,
And about the silvery fountains
   That make sweet melodies !
For the roses in their brightness
   A little song I'd make,
And the lilies in their whiteness
   As they lie upon the lake !

I'd sing of all ——

But before Lucy could say *of all what,* the
baby began to fret and cry. She was tired of
her flowers, tired of the sunshine, and wanted
to go to sleep. So, putting her pencil and
paper back into her pocket, Lucy began to
move the little wagon gently backwards and
forwards to the time her thoughts were so

softly beating, until Hetty's murmurings were lost in sweet baby slumbers.

"It won't do to keep her out here now," Lucy reflected. "She will be sure to take cold, and I may as well take her back to the house and finish my writing another time. I've had a very nice morning any way."

A little pleasure was a great deal to Lucy Lee, and for several days she went around the house as radiant as a sunbeam, though she found no time to study or finish her second composition. She *thought* a great deal, however, and was very hopeful that somehow, in spite of all her discouragements, she should get an education such as she needed to make her happy and fit her to be useful in the world. She knew how to study by herself better than before she went to school, and had as many lessons all marked out and explained as she could learn in some months. If she only found leisure when the days grew longer, she would get along well.

At the breakfast-table one morning Mr. Lee

told Harry and Charley he wished them to sort the potatoes for planting that day. For every bushel he would give them a penny. They could scarcely wait to finish their breakfast, so eager were they to commence the work.

"That's the way you spoil the children," said Mrs. Lee, "hiring them to do whatever they don't like. *My* way is to tell a child what I want, and see that it is done."

"I know it, mother; I know your way; but I haven't travelled so far from childhood yet as not to remember how much easier and pleasanter it is to work with the hope of reward than for fear of punishment. A penny goes a great ways with children to keep them from growing tired and getting discouraged. And it is about the same with grown folks, too, I guess. When I's a young man, I went down to New York once to see what I could see. It was nothing but hurrying and driving there from morning till midnight, just for the hope of gain. I shall never forget it. Men that love the sky and earth and green hills and mountains as well as I do, may be, would stay cheerfully in dusty streets and dark shops just for a penny more profit, just as our boys will stay all day to-day down in the cellar-hole, when the sun shines, and the birds sing so pleasantly above."

Lucy followed her father when he went out to yoke his team for ploughing. "May I help the boys when I get my dishes washed?" she inquired.

"What for, child; don't you have women's work enough to do?"

"I want some money to get me a bottle of ink," she said hesitatingly. "The ink mother made last winter got frozen, and will not write. well. I want some nice and black before I write to Miss Willis."

"If mother can spare you, well and good. If not, never mind it, and I will get you the ink when I go to town."

Lucy hastened to wash her dishes, and make her brothers, bed and her own, before she asked her mother. Mrs. Lee said she might go until it was time to be getting dinner; she should need her then. With a light heart she tied on her hood and pinned a warm blanket round her shoulders, as it was damp in the cellar always. Then she ran quickly to join Harry and Charley in their work. They had two piles sorted already when Lucy got there, to which they called her attention.

"His are the silver-skins, and mine are blue-noses," said Charley. "But what have you come for, Lucy? There ain't a potato more here than we can do ourselves; we are going to put our cents together and get an india-rubber ball, if we get enough."

"I want some money, too," said Lucy. "I haven't had a cent since I sold my hazel-nuts last fall, and we got our school-books."

"What do girls want money for? They don't play ball."

"I know it; but I want some ink, I want it dreadfully. I can't write to Miss Willis with that poor old frozen stuff. It sticks up the steel pens so they will not make a mark."

"Let father have it, then, for his account-book. He always uses a goose-quill, you know," said Harry. "I don't blame you for wanting some good ink to write to Miss Willis with. You may sort the *marinoes*, Lucy, because they are largest and fill up fastest; Charley and I were saving them for the last."

Lucy would not take the advantage of her brothers' generosity, but insisted they would work together on the smaller ones first, then on the larger ones.

"When you do write to Miss Willis," said Harry, "tell her I've read the 'Robinson Crusoe' she gave me three times through, and like it first-rate."

"And that I've painted every soldier in my picture-book with cranberries and indigo till they look as fine as real soldiers, such as we see when we go to training," said Charley. "I wish she'd come back here!"

"I'll write her that, too," replied Lucy; "and that we all wish so."

Talking first about Miss Willis and the school, then about other things, the morning passed away very quickly and pleasantly, though they were handling potatoes in a damp, shady cellar. The spirit with which children labor has often more to do with its ease or heaviness than the labor itself.

"We shall earn about five cents apiece to-day, I guess," said Harry, as he emptied down another bushel measure.

"I'm afraid I sha'n't," said Lucy. "I expect every minute to hear mother call me to help get dinner."

"We'll pick over for you, if she does," said Charley. "It's worth as much to work in the house as to sort potatoes any hour."

The expected call was soon heard, and for the next hour Lucy was as busy as she could be in the kitchen. The boys both petitioned to have her help again in the afternoon; so as soon as the after-dinner work was done she was with **them** again in the cellar, where they amused themselves telling stories and asking puzzling questions until their work was done. The boys received six cents each at evening, and Lucy her bottle of ink, her father finding an opportunity to send for it that very afternoon.

CHAPTER IX.

WHAT leisure Lucy could find for the next few days was spent upon her letter. She wrote a good many things in the first place which she did not like afterwards, and so two or three letters were written before she was satisfied. Miss Willis urged her to say whatever she liked without reserve, but, like many others, Lucy found it very difficult to express what she most wished. It was very easy to write about what had taken place in the neighborhood since she left, and to pen the messages which one and another had sent; but when she came to her own feelings and thoughts, which her friend asked her to speak of freely, it was far more difficult than she had foreseen. She thought she would tell her about her first composition, and how mortified she had felt at her

mother's criticism; then it did not seem quite
right to mention, even though true, her mother's want of interest and sympathy in her
efforts. She decided to say only that she had
made two attempts to write something in verse;
the first was a very lame affair, and the second,
though a little better, was not finished, because,
though she knew well enough what she was
going to say, she could not say it, and have it
sound like what she had written in the first
place.

Had her mother been like Miss Willis, Lucy
would have gone to her, and asked to be advised on two or three points; but she was getting more and more reserved every day, more
reluctant even to communicate her thoughts
and feelings to her natural friend and guide
than to a stranger. A painful consciousness of
not being understood has sealed many a child's
heart besides Lucy Lee's, and left the warm cur-
rents which would gush forth in the sunshine
of love to chill and freeze in hidden depths.

The letter was sealed at last, and sent; and

as the days were now getting longer and warmer, Lucy tried to find a little time to study. She was up very early in the morning, and never lost a moment. Some mornings she had time to read over a page or two of history before her mother called her to dress the children and help about breakfast. Then she would think it over and over as she went about her work, until she knew it perfectly. Other mornings she would have time only for a single paragraph like the following: "The first permanent English settlement in America was made at Jamestown, Virginia, in 1607." And this was repeated softly until it became as familiar as her own name and age. Whenever she went out with the baby, the book was sure to have a hiding-place in a corner of the little wagon, and in that way some new historic fact was often added to her small stock of learning. Few children have either as much fondness for knowledge, or as much perseverance in acquiring it under adverse circumstances, as Lucy had; and if she felt sometimes like giving up the pursuit in despair, it was only days when she felt too sick and weary to make any exertion beyond those absolutely required of her. She had many such days before the summer was over, but with the first hour of strength came back the native courage and resolve.

"I *must*, and *can*, and *will have an education*," she said one day to her mother, in a petulant tone, when chided, as she often was, for taking her book instead of her knitting-work while tending the baby. "My hands are yours, and you manage in one way or another to keep them pretty well filled; but my head is my own, and you cannot control it."

Lucy had never spoken thus to her mother before. Her father, who chanced to overhear the words, opened not his mouth to reprove or approve. But after she had gone to her bed that night, unhappy as she could be, Mr. Lee said to his wife, "You are spoiling that child's disposition by constant fault-finding and opposition. You know as well as I do that over and above her books she does more work than

any other little girl in the neighborhood. I
can't bear to see her young face look so care-
worn; and if you don't let her have her own
way more, I will send her away from home to
school, if I have to sell my last cow for it."

The threat did not, however, do much to
lighten Lucy's daily tasks. With her mother's
hands so full, how could she find time for
study? She did not expect much, but her
heart pleaded most earnestly for more tender
sympathy. It was the want of that which
clouded her young face, and often wet her pillow with bitter tears. It was the want of
what every parent, however poor in worldly
goods, owes a child even before food or
raiment.

Only in the abstract had religion a place in
the home of Lucy Lee. Her parents believed
in the Bible, and taught their children it was
the word of God. But its practical influence
upon their hearts and lives was not manifest.
The candle of the Lord shone not upon them
as upon the tabernacle of the righteous. They

had no altar for morning or evening sacrifice. Whenever there was public worship in the village, they attended, and took their little ones to the Sabbath-school; but latterly they had been deprived of such means of grace. Coldness and indifference to spiritual things seemed to have settled down on the hearts of professing Christians through all the region. They had had no minister for some time, and the parish was too small and poor to make it an object for an aspiring man to abide there.

Happily, among the teachers of Christ are some who esteem souls above earthly gain, who are willing to put on the *likeness* and make self-denial for the cause of their Heavenly Master. One of these came about this time to the little village among the mountains. He had heard of the destitution of gospel privileges there, and how the flock, without a leader and guide, was getting astray. With a heart warm with love, he said: "Let me cast in my lot among you. I am not destitute; those who are, and have families to support, must make stipulations to live. Your little ones need a teacher; let me tell them of the Good Shepherd who leadeth into ' green pastures ' and beside 'still waters.' "

How the hearts of that neglected people went forth to the stranger none can think who have never known similar need and similar unselfishness. Mr. Robbins was a man whose religion was fashioned on the precepts of the New Testament, whose whole nature was warmed and influenced thereby. In the simplicity of his life and character, in his devotion to his Heavenly Father's work, and his love to his fellow-immortals, he was not an unworthy follower of Him who was meek and lowly in heart, and who all His life long went about doing good. The doors of the sanctuary were again thrown open on the Sabbath, meetings for conference and prayer were held in different sections of the parish, and the Sabbath-school was once more thronged with happy children. To train immortal souls for another and a higher life was the work for which the young pastor was enlisted, and he set himself to the work like a . faithful soldier of the Cross.

CHAPTER X.

LOVE begets love. There was not a heart in
the parish that was not moved by the faithful,
earnest exhortations of the new minister. He
did not begin his work by reproaching the
people for their backslidings and shortcomings
in duty; but he called on the weak and wandering to return, like the prodigal of old, to the
fulness of their Father's house. The feast
was waiting for them there. The best robe and
the gold ring were always ready for the erring
child. God's servants were sent with the invitation: "Come! for all things are now ready."
For the weary and heavy laden, for the sick
and sorrowing, for the poor, the lame, and the
blind, for the aged whose feet were treading
the dim evening-way of life, and for the young
in their freshness and vigor, the gospel invita-

tion was sent. Whoever would, might come.
"Eat, O friends! drink abundantly, O be-
loved!" was the Master's welcome to the feast
He had spread.

Under such preaching the church was first
aroused. The language of its members was:
"All we like sheep have gone astray." Many
who had never before felt any personal interest
in the subject began to inquire whether the
gospel call was not to them also. For many
and many a year no such feeling had been
awakened in that community, and the faithful
minister toiled on, humbly and meekly striving
to sow the good seed. He visited from house
to house, and learned the spiritual wants of
many who had never made known such a want
before. He conversed so simply and affection-
ately, none felt as if making known their
thoughts and feelings to a stranger. Even the
children were unawed at his presence, and
loved to listen to his words.

"I tell you, Lucy, I like him first-rate!"
Harry Lee said to his sister, as they were walk-

ing from church one Sabbath afternoon. "He preaches so children can understand him, and not like old Mr. Martin, whose sermons sound to me just like a chapter of Romans."

Mr. Robbins had been preaching from the text: "He shall feed His flock like a shepherd; He shall gather the lambs with His arm, and carry them in His bosom, and shall gently lead those that are with young."

"I like him, too," replied Lucy. "And I feel as though I should like to be carried in the Saviour's arms. I am so tired and unhappy, Harry!" Lucy burst into tears as she spoke.

"I say," said Harry, "if you are tired, let's sit down on that rock there, and wait till father and mother get round with the wagon. You can ride the rest of the way."

Lucy did not wish to ride. She had walked from choice, and she and her brother had taken a foot-path across the fields, which shortened the first part of the way a good deal. She had not been feeling well for some days, and every exertion fatigued her. Little things fretted

her as they had never done before. Even her
father said to her the day before, when she
spoke hastily to one of the children, "I am
afraid you are really growing cross, Lucy!"

"Tired and unhappy!" That was her feeling as nearly as she could express it. But that
was not all. Though scarcely more than ten
years old, Lucy had thought and felt a great
deal. For a long time she had been sensible
of an earnest desire for something she did not
possess. Sometimes it was only pleasant sympathy; sometimes knowledge. Now it was
something beyond and above either of these—
something on which an immortal nature might
feed and rest. Her mind was awakened to a
sense of her lost estate by nature, and of her
need of recovering grace. The plan of salvation had been clearly set forth by the minister
that morning; and in the afternoon the believer's comfort and safety were dwelt upon.

Lucy could no longer say to her conscience
as she had sometimes said before: "I want to
be a Christian, but don't know how;" for the

way had been made plain to her that day through the blood of the Lamb. As she and Harry walked slowly homewards, she felt the necessity of an entire consecration of heart and life. " I will give myself to the Saviour this very night!" was her secret resolve. " I *can* and *must* be a Christian ! "

When supper was over, she went to her chamber and made fast the door. Kneeling down by her low bedside, she said softly: " Dear Saviour, I am a poor, helpless, sin-sick child, and I come to give myself to Thee. Leave me not to perish. I cannot go any longer by myself; take me in Thy strong arms, and carry me safely all the way through life." Those were all the words her lips uttered, but her repentant spirit told all its wants and griefs in such silent language as the Father of Spirits understands and heeds. A few days before Lucy had begun to read the New Testament in course. She had got as far as the eleventh chapter of Matthew, to which she now opened and read. The last verses of the chapter were very sweet: " At that time Jesus answered and said, I thank Thee, O Father, Lord of heaven and earth, because Thou hast hid these things from the wise and prudent, and hast revealed them unto babes. Even so, Father; for so it seemed good in Thy sight. Come unto Me, all ye that labor and are heavy laden, and I will give you rest. Take My yoke upon you, and learn of Me; for I am meek and lowly in heart: and ye shall find rest unto your souls. For My yoke is easy, and My burden is light."

" I think," she said to herself, " as I grow to be a Christian I shall understand things better. Some things I will ask Miss Willis when I write to her again. She is a Christian; I always knew dear Miss Willis was a Christian."

CHAPTER XI.

THAT week Mr. Robbins made his second call at Mr. Lee's. It was Thursday. He had intended to call earlier in the week, but was sent for to attend a funeral at some distance, and only returned the day before. He had noticed Lucy's serious face, both in church and at Sabbath-school, and how attentively she listened to his instructions. He knew her from the description some one had given him, and wished to tell her he had a message from one of her friends for her; but she was not at home when he called first, and so the message was reserved for a second visit.

The gig of the village physician stood at the gate of the cottage when he arrived. Mr. Robbins knocked two or three times before any person came to the door. Mrs. Lee came at last, and her eyes were red with weeping. He inquired if they were ill there, and was told that Lucy, the eldest child, was like to die.

In answer to his inquiries, the mother said she had been a little complaining for a number of days, though no one dreamed of her being seriously ill. She walked from church Sunday, was worse on Monday, and Tuesday broke down entirely. Since Tuesday she had not lifted her head, or scarcely · spoken a word of sense, though she had talked and moaned continually.

Mr. Robbins went in. Doctor King sat by the bedside, holding his patient's pulse, and watching her flushed, fevered countenance. Mr. Lee was near, with the youngest child in his arms, and looked very much troubled.

"Lucy," he said, after rising and greeting the welcome pastor—"Lucy, Mr. Robbins has called to see us. Do you not recognise him?"

Lucy opened her eyes and said: "I am very tired to-day!" then closed them again and moaned as before.

"That's the way with her all the time now," her mother said. "So it was for a day or two before she was taken down, and I drove her round just the same as though she'd been well and strong," and her tears burst forth afresh.

"There's no doubt the child is overdone in mind and body both," the physician said bluntly. "But this is the time for remedies, and not reproaches. Lucy, my child," and the doctor raised her on his strong arm, and put a cup to her lips, "I want you should take this."

"I want to write to Miss Willis, and ask her to explain some things to me," she said, gazing vacantly around. "Can I to-day?"

"Take the drink, and then we'll see how you feel. You shall write as soon as you are able," the doctor said soothingly.

She drank the medicine, and fixed her eyes on Mr. Robbins with a look of intelligent recognition, then smiled faintly and held out her hand.

"I am very sorry to find you so ill," he said,

taking her hand, and speaking in the gentlest tone. "But I hope you will soon be better."

"I want to be a Christian," she said, "but I am so tired now, I cannot think much. Do you think I ever shall learn anything?"

"You know more than a great many grown folks now, Lucy," the doctor said; "and if you'll only keep quiet, and take my medicines, we'll have you able to do what you like in a few days."

After giving the most explicit directions about her medicines, and promising to be there again before night, Doctor King rose to leave.

Mr. Robbins rose also, and speaking a word of hope to the sorrowing parents, exhorting them to look to God in this and every trial, followed the physician from the door. At the gate he inquired the doctor's opinion of the case.

"I don't know which way 'twill go, certainly," he replied. "I am afraid of the brain. There is too much action there altogether. She's always been a wonderful child, though

27

folks ain't apt to see such things at home. But," he added, energetically seizing his bridle-rein, "if there's skill enough in me, I won't lose Lucy Lee. I have a call that must be made this afternoon, then I am coming back to stick to her like a friend. Her mother is a capital nurse as a general thing, but she is half-frightened out of her wits now, and I don't wonder at it."

Thus suddenly was Lucy prostrated on a bed of sickness, perhaps of death. She had her reason only at irregular periods, and not sufficiently at any time to realize the danger of her situation. Hour after hour did her parents bend their ears to listen to her incoherent words, promising themselves and their God, if their child might only be raised up from this sickness, they would be more careful of her strength and more tender of her feelings. How many such painful reflections crowd around the sick-beds of those we love, often too late to test the sincerity of the promises we make for the time to come!

Doctor King could not have bestowed a tenderer care upon an own child than he gave to little Lucy Lee. Day after day, and night after night, he might have been found at the cottage, scarcely leaving her bedside to eat or sleep. The house was thronged with neighbors; but after Thursday no person except the immediate watcher was allowed to enter the sick-room, the physician insisting that her life depended on the most absolute quiet.

No one came oftener to inquire for Lucy than Mr. Robbins; and whenever the doctor's gig was seen at his own door, he was usually the first to ask after the suffering child. "I tell you, sir," said the physician to him one day, "she is a most remarkable little thing. Yesterday she gave me the history of the United States in a nutshell, and to-day she talks about experimental religion like an old Doctor of Divinity. But she grows weaker and weaker every day, and whether there'll be anything left of her when the fever is run out, I can't say."

Prayers were offered in the Sabbath-school for one of their number very near to death, and many of the children wept to think of dear Lucy Lee, who was with them so lately studying the word of God. Many parents, too, forgot their own trifling cares in sympathy with the afflicted ones, and heartfelt petitions were offered to the Throne of Grace that God in his infinite compassion would restore the health of the beloved child.

CHAPTER XII.

AFTER two weeks of most extreme suffering,
Lucy lived, though too weak to raise a finger
or speak even her mother's name. "If they
could keep her from sinking now, she might
recover," the kind physician told her parents;
"but that more vigilant care was requisite than
ever, as she had her reason perfectly, and the
least emotion might overpower her and prove
fatal."

Never was an invalid more tenderly nursed
through long warm days and nights than she.
She realized it all, and though she had no
words to express her feelings, grateful tears
often flowed down her pale, thin cheeks. Her
eyes spoke in silent affection to her father,
mother, and good Doctor King whenever they
served her in any way, and sweet smiles re-

paid them for every effort. It was some time
before she could speak except in monosyllables;
but the thought that she was getting better, and
might soon be well again, swelled every heart
with thanksgiving. Harry and Charley, who
had been very silent and sad since Lucy's illness, were as happy as they could be in the
prospect of her recovery, and did everything
they could to testify their joy and to assist their
mother, who had grown pale with care and
anxiety. The two little girls were taken with
them to the field every morning, and left to
amuse themselves in the shade, while they
hoed corn and potatoes like young heroes.
Never before had the family realized the full
strength of their attachment for one another!
It is often thus; for not until some link of the
household chain is broken, or seems ready to
break, is the full strength of the familiar bond
even conjectured. It is grief and sorrow, not
prosperity and joy, which unite hearts most
firmly.

One day when Lucy was a good deal better,

and able to sit pillowed up in bed and talk a
little, Mr. Lee brought the old family Bible and
sat down to read. It was Sunday, and Harry
and Charley had gone to meeting the first time
since her illness. Lucy had thought of them,
and thought of the Sabbath-school many times
that day, and wondered whether she would
ever be strong enough to go there again. She
had not forgotten the last Sunday she was
there, nor what feelings had urged her on her
return to give herself to the Lord Jesus Christ.
Never had she asked herself whether her offering had been accepted, for she had not once
doubted it. His own words, "Whosoever
cometh to Me I will in no wise cast out," were
implicitly believed. A child's faith is a happy,
blessed surety. Not until the human heart
has grown old and cold in error and false ways
does it learn the deep darkness of doubt.

"I wish you would read to me a little, if
you please, father," Lucy said, as she watched
him intent on the sacred book. "I think it is
a long time since I have heard any reading."

"Four weeks to-day, my child, since you went out to meeting and heard lessons from the Bible. You have passed through a great deal since then, Lucy."

"That was the day I gave myself to the Saviour to be a Christian, father. I did not think it was quite so long ago."

Mr. Lee bowed his head on his hands and wept at Lucy's words. Her mother was much moved also to hear her child, looking still as if on the borders of the grave, speak so frankly of her consecration to God. Her father drew his chair nearer to the bed, and said in a broken voice, "If you are a Christian, Lucy, you will have to teach me; for I have promised, with God's help, to become a Christian too."

"I think it is very easy when one has fully made up their mind," she replied simply. "The last chapter I read in my Testament was the eleventh chapter of Matthew. I thought of it a good deal that night after I went to bed so tired, and my head feeling so badly, and kept repeating the last verses to myself. I think they are beautiful."

Mr. Lee turned to it, and read the whole chapter aloud. "My yoke is easy, and My burden is light," he repeated as he closed the book. Then he said solemnly: "Mother, you and I had more need to learn of Him who is meek and lowly in heart than our child; let us take His yoke upon us, and begin here together the Christian life."

Beside Lucy's bed they knelt down and pledged themselves to "walk in newness of life" the remainder of their earthly pilgrimage. Thanksgiving for the Lord's goodness in preserving the life of their child mingled freely in the prayer of consecration. It was a heart-melting season to them all. Tears ran like rain down Lucy's thin cheeks, but they were tears of joy and gladness.

"We cannot help being happy now," she said, when her mother bent over her to wipe the tears from her eyes, and bid her keep quiet

28

and not get over-tired. "I know we shall be a happy family hereafter," and mother and daughter exchanged kisses of affection.

CHAPTER XIII.

MR. ROBBINS called at the cottage again on Monday. He had been at the door a number of times, sometimes bringing a little gift of oranges or apples for Lucy, but had never entered since that first week of her illness. Now he brought a basket of early strawberries, for which he had sent to the city with the doctor's assurance that they would not hurt her. Mr. and Mrs. Lee felt very grateful to him for his interest and kindness.

Lucy had no recollection whatever of his first visit to her sick-bed; no recollection of anything, indeed, which happened during the two first weeks of her illness. But she was very glad to see him now, and answered all the questions he asked respecting her thoughts and feelings, with a modesty and intelligence very

pleasant to hear. Her simple story, how she
carried all her pain and weariness of heart with
her to the Saviour, never doubting His faithful promise to give her *rest*, affected him much.

"Did you think of that sweet promise to the
young, Lucy, 'I love them that love Me, and
those who seek Me early shall find Me?'" the
minister asked.

"No, sir; I did not seek Him. I only gave
myself to Him, I think, when He came to me
in my weakness and sadness."

Nothing could have been more satisfactory
than this unaffected tale of experience; and
when Mr. Robbins asked her if she had any
doubt of Christ's acceptance of her, she looked
up in surprise and said, "Were His promises
ever known to fail?"

"No, God be thanked, never!" was the
fervent rejoinder. "*Not one of all His precious
promises!* Cling to them still, Lucy, and you
will always walk in the light of the Sun of
Righteousness. All the promises of God are
'yea and amen' for ever."

Mr. Lee came in from his work while the pastor was thus speaking. In the fulness of his heart he said: " The Lord hath done wonderful things for us here, whereof we are glad." It was the first intimation Mr. Robbins had had of the change in the father's or mother's feelings, and his joy could scarcely find utterance.

" The one hundred and third psalm is yours emphatically," he said, reaching up and taking the Bible from the shelf.

Mr. Lee asked him to read it, and pray with them also, which he did from the fulness of his heart. The prayer, like the psalm, was all praise and thanksgiving. The little farmhouse was no longer a home of sorrow or sighing, or of poverty and repining. Its inmates had found the unsearchable riches of Christ, and were rejoicing in hope of their heavenly inheritance.

Before Mr. Robbins left, he drew his chair close to Lucy's bedside, and said: " I have been keeping a message for you some time, from a friend at the West. I don't know whether I ought to deliver it to-day or not, since you have had so much fatigue already."

"I do not feel much tired," she said, her face all aglow with a sudden pleasure. "I have but *one* friend at the West, Mr. Robbins, and do you know her?"

"If you have *but one*, I think it quite certain I do," he replied, smiling. "She gave me so faithful a description of yourself, that was before your sickness, that I had no difficulty in knowing you the first time I saw you at church. Miss Willis's message was this, that while I remained here you should allow me to have a little oversight of your studies, as you would let her if she were near. You are not well enough to think about it yet, but when you get stronger you must let me come and hear your lessons occasionally."

"I should be very glad," she answered, with pleasure beaming brightly in her pale face, "but I may not have much time to study even when I am well enough. I have been sick so long, mother will need me if I am ever strong again. She has had a very hard time."

" Don't speak of that now," interrupted Mrs. Lee. "If you are ever able to study again, you shall have all the time I can possibly spare. But Doctor King says you must not look in a book until he has taken you to ride, and tried your strength."

Lucy could not recover from the surprise of knowing that Mr. Robbins was a friend of dear Miss Willis. She wished to ask many questions about it, but hesitated, as though there might be some impropriety in her making inquiries.

"I will tell you all about it some time," Mr. Robbins said, reading her thoughts aright; "but I see you are too tired for any further conversation to-day. Keep up good courage, and may God bless you, and soon restore you to perfect health, my friend's dear young friend, and my own!"

CHAPTER XIV.

WITH all the care of her friends, Lucy did not recover so fast as had been hoped and expected. The Doctor gave her all the medicines to strengthen her she could bear, but her limbs were too weak to take a step for a long time. Every morning her father took her in his arms and set her in the rocking-chair before the window, where she could hear the birds sing, and get a scent of the sweet summer air. But she would soon get weary, and ask to be taken back to bed. Her hands were thin and paler even than her cheeks; they were scarcely strong enough to raise her food to her mouth, after it was carefully cut and prepared.

"I don't see why in the world you don't get an appetite and grow stout," Doctor King said to her one morning, entering while she was sitting over her breakfast. "I thought before this time you'd be hungry enough to eat shingle nails; and here you are again turning away from broiled robin and strawberries. How far can you walk?"

"To the bed, if I hold on to the chairs, and don't fall down by the way," she replied, laughing.

"And that's just what she did yesterday, Doctor," her mother interposed. "I heard something or other drop in here, and came and found her flat on the floor, and whiter than a sheet."

"Good business that, when you and I have been nursing her for weeks, as child was never nursed before! What ails you, Lucy?"

"Miss Wayland sent her down some currant wine this morning, and I tried to have her take a spoonful or so, but she wouldn't till she'd asked you. What do you think about it?" said Mrs. Lee.

"Guess if you bitter it with one of these powders, she won't be likely to drink enough

of it to hurt her. Good old port is what she
wants, but we can't get anything of the sort up
here better than steeped logwood. I came
down in the covered gig this morning, and my
wife charged me to bring Lucy up to help us
eat lamb and green peas for dinner. What do
you say to it? Will you go?"

"I should like to very much, if I could,"
was Lucy's reply.

"What's to hinder?"

"I can't walk a step yet by myself;
and ——"

"And what then? Your father and mother,
with my help, might manage to lift you into
the carriage; and my wife and I, with big
black Phil, will try to get you out, somehow."

Lucy laughed again, remembering how little
Harry had taken her alone that very morning
from the bed to the chair, and said she was as
light as a feather.

Her mother, well pleased at the thought of
having her ride, began to make her ready.
When her shawl was pinned on, her bonnet

tied, and a glass of the bittered wine drunk, the doctor took her in his arms and carried her to the carriage, her mother following with pillow and blanket. But the doctor said Lucy was going to ride in his lap, as the jolting of the gig wouldn't do her any good. So in Doctor King's strong arms, Lucy took the first ride after her long sickness.

Mrs. King met them at the door, and took the invalid from her husband's arms to her own, and laid her softly on her own bed, that she might rest a little while before dinner. A great stuffed easy chair, with a footstool before it, was placed for her at the dinner-table, and Lucy felt very comfortable, and not as tired as she had expected. After dinner she had a pillow upon the sofa, and Mrs. King brought her books and pictures to look at, and did all she could to make her feel at ease and happy. They had a large and well-furnished house, very different from the plain little farm-house of Mrs. Lee, with its almost naked rooms; but Lucy was envious of nothing she saw—not even the beautiful books, the finest by far she had ever seen.

Mrs. King urged her to stay over night, but Lucy was certain her mother would feel anxious if she did not get home. The doctor thought so too, as he had promised to have her there at four in the afternoon, or before dewfall; but he said he would bring her again whenever his wife signified she had an extra dinner cooking.

That was Doctor King's way to talk, and everybody in the parish knew and loved his hearty, cheerful ways, though he was sometimes accused of telling plain truths in a blunt way.

Lucy got home safely, and felt no worse for her ride and visit. Her mother said she had had a long lonely day, and was glad to have her back where she could hear her voice and run and look at her occasionally while she was at her work. The little ones pressed around her too, and Lucy felt very thankful for her humble home and so many friends to love her. A great change had come over that home in a few weeks. Every evening the voice of prayer and praise arose from thence to heaven; and tones softer and gentler than before were heard throughout the day. The youngest children seemed to be conscious of some change, and were less noisy and turbulent than before. "Sissy is sick, and we must be quiet and good," was little Mabel's oft-repeated injunction. Religion softens and refines the harshest natures. As in the hands of the skilful gardener the sweetest flowers and choicest fruits are often made to appear on the thorniest stocks, so will Divine grace transform the natural heart, and cause it to bring forth the pleasant fruits of righteousness.

The next time Mr. Robbins came he brought Lucy something sweeter even than the fruits or flowers he had sent before. It was a note from Miss Willis, directed, "To dear Lucy Lee, if living." Mr. Robbins had written to her of Lucy's dangerous illness, and the tidings had called forth the tenderest expression of her loving heart.

"I must write you a few lines, darling Lucy," she said, "though I write with fear and trembling lest your eyes should never see the tearful words I am penning. It makes me very sad to feel this sickness of yours may be unto death; not that it is a sad thing for the children of God to die. To them it is but a removal from one country to another—from a country of pain, sorrow, and death, to one of immortal life, and health, and joy. I think I conversed less with my beloved pupils last winter about that immortal country than I should have done. I feel now, when I hear that one of them—one so very dear to me—is on the borders of the unseen world, that I was too anxious to fit them for life and usefulness in this world, and too careless about their preparation for the next. If God raises you up to health again, dear Lucy, will you not make an entire consecration of yourself to His service? I think I have written to you before that, with all your thirstings and aspirings, you will never rest satisfied with anything earthly. Mr. Robbins wrote me that he easily recognised you from my description, and felt sure you were a seeker after religion. He is a good man, and a very dear friend of mine. When we parted here, I charged him with a message for you, and am sorry he had not the opportunity to deliver it before your sickness. I give him another charge now not to forget your immortal need. He will be your friend and teacher. Your letter did me much good, and I hope to receive many more from you in health and strength. I shall write again as soon as I hear how you are. Until then rest assured of the warmest love of your friend,

" A. WILLIS."

Lucy could not hide her tears while reading the kind words of her dear teacher and friend. Before the note was finished, she was sobbing audibly. Mr. Robbins was conversing with her mother, and neither appeared to take notice of her emotion. When she had recovered her composure, she said, " I would like to answer this letter, if I were only strong enough."

"Let me write for you," Mr. Robbins said, kindly drawing near to her; "you may trust me to tell her anything you wish me to. It was through her influence, Lucy, I was persuaded to come to this place and try to do good. I preached more than two years at the West, where she is now teaching. When my health failed there, and I was ordered to return to New England, she spoke of this quiet little place up among the mountains, and urged me to come hither. She had just returned from here herself, and spoke warmly of the people, and of their spiritual necessities, as well as of the salubrity of the climate. Had not my health failed, Miss Willis and I were to have been married soon; but that event is postponed until I am able to return to my former field of labor, or we shall be able to decide upon a new one in a more healthy locality. I hope, now I have told you this, you will not hesitate to send any messages you like, until you are able to write to your friend yourself."

"Will you read this, sir?" she said, quietly

putting the note into his hand. "Tell her I thank her for it, and I think you will know what else I wish most to say. And Mr. Robbins," Lucy colored and hesitated, "I wish you would some time bring dear Miss Willis back again among the mountains." Tears filled her eyes as she spoke.

Mr. Robbins observed them, and answered caressingly, "She shall come, if our lives are spared, my dear child. She has a sister here, you know, and many friends besides me."

The note which Lucy put in his hand, he read silently, and said as he returned it, "What I shall write, Lucy, will make our friend very happy."

30

CHAPTER XIV.

IT was autumn before Lucy was able to run about again in her old way. That summer was the pleasantest one of her life, however, for though languid and weak in body, the mind was serene and peaceful. All its old unrest was calmed by the thought that God would guide her in the right way; that He who sees the end from the beginning knew what was best for his short-sighted child. She fretted no more about her books, but was content to learn lessons of patience and self-denial. Every one was kind to her, and she felt her heart drawn out in love to all her fellow-creatures. She sewed and knitted, and did light work around the house as fast as she got strength. The doctor did not think her able to study, but he took her often to ride with him instead; and when he found how much she loved the mountains, he made frequent errands to their summits, and sometimes to the villages beyond. Lucy felt very grateful for his many kindnesses to her, though he would never allow her to say a word about it. "Wasn't it pleasanter for a person who had to go night and day to have company sometimes?" he inquired. "No man could live by chewing his own cud always. His wife was more afraid of the mountains than of bears, and he wanted some one to speak to occasionally. Moreover, old Jack was always ready to run away, if he stopped a minute for hazel-nuts, or mountain raspberries, which were very good in their season, and which often he had to pass without picking, because he had nobody to hold the reins for him."

So it was on account of the doctor's fondness for company in his excursions, and old Jack's unsteadiness, which no mortal ever suspected before, or for some other reason quite as enigmatical, that Lucy found herself often enjoying the glorious scenery of the mountains which skirted her valley home. It was more than enjoyment to her; it was a sweet, calm rapture, such as a little flower might be supposed to feel in the hour of its unfolding.

Many grave discussions attended these excursions, for the doctor loved nothing better than to drop a weighty thread occasionally into her child mind, and sound its depths. There was a freshness and vigor in the thoughts evoked from thence which he liked better than all the logic of the schools. The simple earnestness with which she brought her own reasons and convictions to weigh against his cavils simply amused him at first, until the force of her arguments filled him with surprise.

"Who has taught you all these things?" he inquired of her one day when he had been drawing her out on the subject of religion. "Who told you how to answer an old sceptic who doubts everything almost, except his own existence?"

Lucy blushed and hesitated. Her face was

more of a puzzle to the old man than her words.

"I think the Holy Spirit teaches me the little I know," she answered meekly.

"What makes you think so, child? The Holy Spirit teaches me nothing of the sort."

"Perhaps you don't go to His school," was the naive reply. "It is only lately I have understood anything in this way. You know the Bible says: 'The natural man receiveth not the things of the Spirit of God, for they are foolishness unto him: neither can he know them, because they are spiritually discerned.' That is why I think, when I understand things now which were all dark to me before, that the Spirit teaches me."

" *They shall all be taught of God,*" mused the doctor in an undertone, and a long silence ensued. Then Lucy ventured to say:

"I think if you would talk to Mr. Robbins on the subject, he would be able to explain some things to you more plainly."

"Pho! Mr. Robbins teaches as he has been

taught, I suppose. I don't care a fig about seminary theology any way."

"But he is a good man," persisted Lucy.

"Yes; there you have me again. No one can dispute Mr. Robbins being a good man who takes note of his daily life; and that's the preaching that tells. Not the speaking with the tongues of men or of angels, which without charity is no more than sounding brass or tinkling cymbals. Mr. Robbins practises all he preaches; and does not, like the evil shepherds, '*Eat the fat and clothe himself with the wool*' of the Lord's poor. I know something about him myself, Lucy. There are my two patients up at the poor-house, whom he visits oftener than I do, and carries them better medicines than anything in my saddle-bags, by all odds. Last week he took warm flannel for the old woman with rheumatism, and fresh meat and peaches for the young one in consumption. I caught him in the distribution, and he apologized and stammered as though he thought himself verily guilty of what I accused him, namely, *the intent to steal away my practice.*"

" But he knew you were not in earnest, doctor ! "

" *How* did he know it ? "

" Just as *I* know, when you come for me to ride, and say it's because you can't trust old Jack with the buggy when the sun shines; and just as I know too, that while you call yourself an unbeliever, you are *almost* a Christian."

" I would to God I were altogether one, my child," he answered solemnly, " in heart and life, a sincere, humble Christian ! "

" Jesus Christ is the way," Lucy said, looking up to him with a face beaming with gladness. " You will find it a very easy, pleasant way."

" Not as easy as you imagine for an old sinner like me, who had rather go about establishing his own righteousness, than trusting in the merits of the Son of God. I know it is a way that opens wide unto the young."

They had no more conversation that day, for they had just reached the door of Lucy's home. But the doctor took her from the carriage with even more than his customary tenderness, and said, "You shall be my teacher henceforward, my good little girl."

Lucy could not dismiss the doctor's words from her mind. She thought of the sad tone with which he said, "*Not as easy as you imagine.*" It was so unlike his usual cheerful voice, that it went to her very heart. No one could have been kinder than Doctor King had been to her ever since her sickness, no gentle woman more sympathizing in her hours of pain and weakness. Now he was weary and heavy-laden perhaps, just as she had been when she first longed to be lifted in the arms of the Good Shepherd. How gladly would Lucy have taken him by the hand, and said, "Come to my Saviour and he will give you rest."

"What can I do for him!" she often thought as she went round the house, a shadow graver than usual. She thought at last; and when she went up to her little chamber that night, she prayed as she had seldom prayed before, that the blindness might be removed from her dear friend's eyes; that he might see the way of salvation plainly, through a crucified Redeemer.

31

CHAPTER XV.

THE next time Doctor King came to take Lucy to ride, he said to her, "I haven't found the way you spoke of yet, my child—the way to be a Christian."

"Have you asked?" she inquired.

"I have asked my own reason and heart, but they give me no assurance."

"If we were riding a way we did not know and should get lost, would you ask your own reason the right way, or look for a guide or guide-board?"

"We might not be able to find either, Lucy."

"But we can always find them on the way from earth to heaven; and we have only to inquire, to be led aright."

"How can you prove it?"

" By this little guide-book," she said, taking her Testament from her pocket, and opening to the seventh chapter of Matthew. " It is written here, ' Ask, and it shall be given you; seek, and ye shall find; knock, and it shall be opened unto you. For every one that asketh, receiveth; and he that seeketh, findeth; and to him that knocketh, it shall be opened.' *Every one*, you see, doctor. It don't say a few, or a good many, but every one who wishes."

The doctor sat watching her thin, earnest face as she spoke. " I see you believe that guide implicitly," he said, as she looked up in his face for some reply.

" Which way should I turn if I didn't? " she answered sadly. " Oh, Doctor King! don't you believe this precious guide? "

" I am not certain. If I really did believe it, should I stand doubting and hesitating as I do now, my child? "

" I don't know," she said, and tears filled her eyes as she spoke. " But if you don't feel quite sure, the Saviour will not leave you. He will come and stand at the door of your heart and ask to be let in. I think he is knocking there now, and I know you will open it to him; won't you?" and the tears, which a moment before had gathered in her eyes, now fell thickly.

No one would have believed the soft, tremulous voice that answered, "I'm a hardened old fellow, Lucy, but I will try," belonged to the village doctor; no one who had never heard it in the hour of anguish, or death, when the usual blunt-toned physician yielded to the tender, sorrowing friend. Lucy's little ungloved hand was laid gently in the doctor's great, broad palm, and the smile that lighted up her features looked not unlike the rainbow which shines from a summer cloud. She did not say his words made her glad, but every expression of her face, every tone of her voice, testified it more plainly than any words.

The doctor had a number of calls to make that afternoon, and it was nearly night when

Lucy reached home, happier than she had **ever** felt before, at the close of a pleasant day.

It was soon remarked throughout the parish that Doctor King **was** interested in religion. His attendance upon the meetings for prayer became frequent, while the seriousness of his countenance indicated a solemn questioning of heart. No one approached him on the subject, fearful, perhaps, of disturbing the silent operations of the Holy Spirit. Even Mr. Robbins forbore questioning, though he was often borne on his spirit to the throne of love and grace. Only a warmer grasp of the hand when they met, and on one occasion an involuntary "God help you, my dear sir," told the devoted pastor's sympathy with the awakened man. A more demonstrative character, or an intellect of less scope, he would have approached differently; but in no other way could he so effectually have opened the interior passages of the doctor's confidence, and brought him to unbosom his new wants and resolves. Then, as brother stands by brother in the hour of trial and condemnation, as petition after petition is drawn up and presented for his pardon, so did the affectionate young minister stand with words of encouragement, and cheering promises of abundant, free forgiveness through the great atoning sacrifice.

"The same way of salvation our little invalid has been preaching to me for days and weeks," the doctor said. Then he told of the many conversations he had had with Lucy in their rides together, and how earnestly she had labored to lead him from the paths of unbelief.

"There is no other name given among men whereby we can be saved," said Mr. Robbins, solemnly. "The oldest divine, and the youngest child taking the first steps in the Christian course, can speak of no other than the Living Way. Lucy was wonderfully prepared to find that way a way of pleasantness and peace."

"That child would make an able evangelist, Mr. Robbins."

"I hope to see her educated for a teacher,' was his reply. "I have only been waiting for you to say she is sufficiently strong, to renew my offers of assistance."

It was not long after the foregoing conversation, that Doctor King arose in a meeting for conference and prayer, and spoke in a subdued tone of the dealings of God with his soul, and of his wish and determination in future to live as became a man who had put on Christ. His words were few, but there was something in his manner which carried conviction to all present, that his was no hasty resolve, born in the impulse of a moment, to melt away with time, but a deliberate, sanctified purpose, stretching forward into the long years of eternity. Many a heart was gladdened, and many eyes made tearful by that simple testimony of the parish physician, who, of all men among them, was the best beloved. Many a mother in that congregation whose little one had closed its eyes in her kind arms in the slumber that knows no earthly awaking, wept at the remembrance of his tender sympathy; while her heart swelled with thanksgiving, that his own strong spirit had found something to comfort and stay itself upon at last.

Doctor King's conversion seemed to be the last drop of the pleasant revival shower—the crowning sheaf of a precious, harvest summer.

CHAPTER XVI.

THE autumn came with its crimson woods and golden harvests. Never had the fields of the husbandmen ripened in richer plenty. Never, from that little parish among the mountains, had so many hearts been ready to offer thanksgiving for all God's mercies.

"As the Lord hath prospered us, we ought to give for the support of the gospel in our midst," said one and another new-born soul. "The laborer is worthy of his hire." A meeting was called, and it was voted unanimously to ascertain whether Mr. Robbins could be induced to settle among them for such salary as they could offer. Doctor King was foremost in the enterprise, and pledged himself for one-fourth of whatever sum the parish would agree to raise. With this promise, four hundred dollars were speedily voted, and a committee appointed to wait upon the pastor of their choice.

Mr. Robbins was taken by surprise. He had never dreamed of a call to settle in the little obscure parish, to which Christian love and charity had first directed his steps. He wanted time to reflect upon it; time, too, to consult another whose life-lot was to be linked with his own. He felt that the people had pledged themselves for a sum greater than in their humble circumstances they could afford, and he told them so frankly. But the people were willing to make any self-denial rather than be deprived again of the preaching of the gospel.

Mr. Robbins had just opened a school in the village for an autumn term, and had had several applications from neighboring parishes to receive pupils. The thought occurred to him, " What, after all, if the Lord have been leading me in a way that I knew not of, and this be the place appointed for me! What, if for this same purpose, he took away my health and destroyed my present hopes of usefulness in the broader field upon which I had entered, that I might, all my life long, preach the gospel to the poor, and train youthful feet for the paths of life and immortality ! If so, am I not ready ? 'Tis a humble lot, but so was my master's."

A number of weeks elapsed before Mr. Robbins replied to the call; weeks of doubt and anxiety to himself, as well as to the parishioners. He made it a subject of daily prayer, until the way became plain before him. He was not one who looked lightly upon the duties and responsibilities involved in the pastoral office; neither did he believe in the growing custom of changing or breaking up for trivial reasons, the settled sacred relation of pastor and people.

"Have you made up your mind to abide with us on such poor terms as we can offer ?" was the inquiry of Doctor King, one evening when they met.

"Until I die, if the Lord will," was the warm, heart-gushing response.

It was speedily communicated to the waiting parish, and received with great joy.

Our reader may like to see the extract from a letter, which was not without its influence upon the foregoing decision:

"Since you urge me to speak my mind freely," the writer said, "and ask whether I am prepared to spend my life among the hills of Vermont, I can only reply, if there be your call, and there your work, I shall rejoice at the one, and be ready to share in the other. I should love to live among the mountains far better than in the city, or on the prairie, if we may only be as useful there as elsewhere. It seems to me our souls, as well as our bodies, grow more vigorous in such a clear, calm atmosphere; and I am confident we should enjoy more of each other's society there than in this busy frontier city. I shall leave my school here with reluctance; but what you write of my Vermont pupils, and the prospect of a permanent school there, will lighten my sorrow. I am very glad that Lucy is so far recovered, and able to study a little. The influence she exerted on Doctor King scarcely surprised me; for such warm, earnest natures as hers, are born to exert an influence. I hope, if you decide to remain, we shall be able to assist her very much. Give much love to her, and say what you please about the probability of my seeing her soon."

Talk about an ordination soon began to be heard. Such an event had taken place but once in the parish, and that was long years before, when the "old folks" were young. For various reasons Mr. Robbins wished to have it postponed until Christmas; one was, his school would not be out until November; another, he had a journey to make which would require an absence of a number of weeks.

Every one guessed the purpose of his journey, though no one was specially informed but Lucy Lee, who never told what she knew

of the matter. Words would hardly express
the delight which that intelligence afforded her,
for though, since Mr. Robbins's promise, she
had looked forward with hope to a meeting with
her beloved friend at some future time, it had
never occurred to her that she would return to
make her home in their little mountain village.
She had supposed it very certain that after the
confirmation of Mr. Robbins's health, he would
go back again to his former field of labor.
His consent to abide with them was therefore
almost as much of a marvel to her as a joy.

Harry and Charley Lee both attended the
autumn school, but as Lucy was not able, she
was as contented and happy as possible with
her lessons at home. Though she still did all
she could to assist her mother with the house-
work, sewing and knitting, and found but little
time for study, everything went pleasantly and
harmoniously now. Her mother had reproached herself too much during her daughter's illness, to longer oppose her tastes, if she still
failed to comprehend them. So Lucy studied

grammar or history, or wrote out her poetic fancies, whenever she found opportunity. Mr. Robbins came as often as he could find time, to encourage and assist her in her studies, and sometimes took away with him a composition which he failed to return. Doctor King came as usual to take her to ride, and one day stopped on their return to speak a word with her mother.

The word was spoken in the doctor's own way. "His wife was tired of being so much alone," he said, "and wished him to call and ask Mrs. Lee's consent for Lucy to come and spend a while with them. There was a whole library of books at her disposal, a room full of medicine if she should happen to need it, and she might take all the knitting and sewing from home she wished to do. How could Mrs. Lee object?"

She could not, with so many advantages held out to her child, though the thought of parting with her for a single day was a sore trouble to her now. Lucy felt this, and said she thought she had better not go. But her mother said if her father were willing, she would not think of keeping her at home on her own account, when a short visit might do her a great deal of good. Luckily she could hear from her every day by the boys when they came from school.

So Doctor King went away with some encouragement, if he came again the next week, Lucy would accompany him home.

At the appointed time he made his appearance, and Lucy, with a little bag of clothes on her arm, and her portfolio tied up in a newspaper in her hand, kissed her mother and the two little ones, then with tears in her eyes took her seat beside the doctor in the familiar buggy.

The doctor wrapped her carefully with the robes, and began to talk to her in a lively tone to make her forget she was leaving home. He told her his wife was tired to death of having never a child nor a chick in the house, except old black Phillis, to speak to when he was gone, and had been to work and fixed her up a nice warm room, where she could read and study and sleep as much as she pleased. The doctor told her only the truth; and Lucy found on her arrival as warm a welcome as she could possibly have wished, and after a day or two she began to feel at home and comfortable.

Mr. Robbins came to see her very soon, and said if Doctor King thought it would not hurt her, he would like to have her come into school a little while every afternoon, and recite arithmetic with the class. The school was only a few steps across the street. Lucy found it very pleasant; and after a few days' trial of her strength, was a regular attendant until its close.

CHAPTER XVII.

THOUGH Mr. and Mrs. Lee and the little ones missed Lucy very much at home, they could not think of depriving her of the advantages so unexpectedly offered. Doctor King insisted that if Mr. Robbins continued his school through the winter, she should remain with them, and attend. They would look after her health as carefully as though she were their own child. With this understanding and promise she went home to spend the vacation, while Mr. Robbins went away to the West.

One clear, bright, December morning, when Lucy had been home about four weeks, she ran to the window at the sound of sleigh bells, and saw Dr. King's horse and cutter stopping before the gate. The doctor was not driving, and a second glance told her it was Mr. Robbins and a lady, "*his wife*," he said, as Lucy met them at the door, and was clasped fondly in the arms of her dear old teacher. They had reached the village the evening before, and were stopping at Dr. King's until their own parsonage-house was ready for them.

Mrs. Robbins was going to spend the first day with her sister, and Dr. King had insisted they should bring Lucy back with them at night, so they called in the morning to bid her be ready.

It was only a few days before the ordination, and the time passed very pleasantly. The school at the new parsonage opened then, and Lucy became a daily pupil. Mrs. Robbins presented her with a number of school-books, more, Lucy thought, than she should ever find time to study. She was mistaken, however, for every month found her making steady advancement. She had some interruptions. There were days when she was not well, and then the doctor would not allow her to go to school. There were seasons of sickness, too, at the cottage at home, and Lucy was always there, a patient nurse and most affectionate watcher. There were other seasons besides, when the labor and care fell too heavy on her mother, and at such times she would go home to divide the weariness and toil.

She was better for these interruptions, stronger in head and heart; better in health, too, it may be, though still very slender and delicate. Her constitution never seemed to quite recover from that first severe shock of illness, and her friends watched over her with the tenderest care.

Lucy carried every doubt and difficulty to Mrs. Robbins, as she had done to dear Miss Willis of old, and found in her the same indulgent, sympathizing friend and helper. And so months and years passed away, and the little parsonage school among the mountains grew to be one of the fixed institutions of the State. Pupils from distant sections flocked in, until there was no more room to receive them. When the parsonage was full, Doctor King took a few boarders; among them was a nephew of his, fitting for the University.

Morton King was a youth of unusual promise, and his influence was soon felt throughout the whole school. Every class with which he was associated, seemed stimulated by his superior scholarship; and as he had always a word of help and encouragement for those who needed them, he was regarded with the highest favor. No one was jealous of his fine talents; no one could have been jealous or envious of one who bore himself so meekly among his fellow students, and was always stimulating them to industry, and trying to do them good. To Lucy, who was just commencing the study of the classics, he was a most valuable assistant. Doctor King's little sitting-room rang at evening with their Latin declensions and conjugations, until his wife declared it was almost as bad as reading the labels in the apothecary's shop. Morton and Lucy led their classes, and were admitted to be the best scholars in the school.

As the cares of her family increased Mrs. Robbins began to give Lucy the oversight of her younger classes, until she grew in time to be the regular assistant pupil-teacher, and received pay for her services. Her proficiency was now more rapid than ever before, for while her earlier lessons were in constant review, her progress was still onward. She was an excellent mathematician, learned the languages with facility, and at fifteen would write a theme or essay which both Mr. Robbins and Doctor King declared fit for a college examination. Occasionally in the poets' corner of one of the State newspapers appeared articles which the editor pronounced "Gems." No one but Lucy and Mrs. Robbins knew anything of their authorship.

At length, one of the metropolitan magazines offered prizes for the best tales and poems which should be offered within two months. Mrs. Robbins whispered to Lucy, "Now is *your* time to enter the field! There will be a hundred aspirants; try with the rest. Your name need not go before the public unless you desire it."

Lucy lent all her strength to the effort, and surpassed even the expectations of her friend and adviser. When, some weeks after, word came that the "Green Mountain Poetess" had won the prize for the second best article, Lucy's heart leaped as it had never done since that May morning so long ago, when she made her first attempt at authorship. She had not forgotten that morning, and would never forget the joy she felt while running down the old staircase to read the successful effort to her mother, and the grief and mortification that followed. Many years had passed since—happy, pleasant years; but those words, "Never let me hear any more such nonsense," would not fade from her recollection. She had written much since then, but never had a word or line of it all been forced upon her mother's notice; for though Mrs. Lee was now one of the kindest, most self-denying of mothers, her taste for literature had in no wise changed.

In the little pasteboard box, up in the drawer of the pine-table at home, was Lucy's first poem, **torn** apart in a moment of humiliation and keen resentment, then laid carefully aside for an hour of triumph. That hour had now come, **but** the resentment had long since passed away, and there was not even triumph in her heart, only a soft, quiet **joy,** as she went and put the letter, with the bank-note which accompanied it, into the hands of her mother. "I don't want the money," she said, with a quivering lip. "I earn all I need in school, and Doctor King will not take a cent for my board. Take it to get things for yourself, and Ruth, and little Hetty."

Both **Mr. and Mrs.** Lee were delighted with this proof of their daughter's talent, though, had the latter spoken her mind freely about the successful poem, it would probably have been like this: "Only some nonsense about the mountains which I never did nor ever can understand."

CHAPTER XVIII.

Lucy's success as a poetess was soon whispered through the school and the village. Her friends congratulated her; and some of them repeated in substance what the editor had written in his letter, that if she gave her attention to literature, a world of fame might lie before her.

Nothing sounds so sweetly in a young author's ear as fame; and Lucy listened to the words of her friends with a new and delicious sensation at her heart. She saw only a flower-strewn way, leading upwards. To the eye of imagination that way had neither thorn nor weariness, and she longed to enter upon it and press forward; but the labor of her classes, together with her own regular studies, left very little time for efforts of imagination.

Only one circumstance damped the pleasure she felt at her literary success; and though she scarcely admitted it even to herself, that one at times lay heavy on her heart. One of her friends and schoolmates, who had always been first to express joy whenever she succeeded in any undertaking, had no word of congratulation for her now, when all besides were making professions of gladness. Morton King not only avoided mentioning it himself, but looked troubled when others spoke of it in his presence. No one noticed this circumstance, perhaps, but Lucy; but she had grown so accustomed to his ways, so familiar with his likes and dislikes, in the two years they had passed together, she felt she could not be mistaken. That Morton was secretly dissatisfied she was certain, though for what reasons she puzzled herself in vain to discover. Sometimes she resolved to ask him, and thus put an end to her doubts; but whenever she attempted to speak about it, delicacy or pride prevented, until a feeling of embarrassment and restraint began to take the place of mutual confidence and esteem. Once or twice Lucy fancied he was going to speak to **her on the** subject, when something prevented; and now the term was fast drawing to a close, and Morton was going away to return no more. -

"I would give anything to know what it is," Lucy said to herself one evening when she had taken her books to her own room to study the morrow's lessons. "I would like to know whether he is really displeased with me, or is only *in the blues* about going away, as his uncle says. He doesn't seem offended, but so changed. I am afraid it is about that magazine article, and I would a thousand times never have written it than to have pained him in any way. Morton **has** been as kind to **me** as a brother, ever since he came."

Lucy's heart spoke the simple truth. Much pleasure as that little poem had given her, she would much rather not have written it, or even that it should have failed of success altogether, than have wounded the schoolmate whose assistance and friendship she had prized so highly.

In the midst of her reflections on the subject, and before her books were opened, she heard the quick step and lively voice of Doctor King at her door.

"Come out, Lu! come quickly," he said, "and help Morton through a page or two of Virgil. Somehow or other, he has got lost in that big wooden horse of Minerva's, and in the midst of so many Grecian youths forgets he is a Trojan."

"Now, Doctor King, that is *my lesson*, and not his," Lucy replied, laughing, as she made haste to open the door. "It is I who have that story of Eneas to translate to-night. Morton knows it all."

"Anyhow, he is out here puzzling over it, and looking sorely bewildered. I thought it was he who needed help, and as I had to go down to old Mrs. Hicks to bring home my wife, and couldn't set him right myself, you should try what you can do."

"What a great tease your uncle is!" Lucy said, as she deposited her heavy dictionary on the stand, and sat down with Virgil in her hands in a seat near by. "I don't see how he discovered the subject of my lesson, to-night."

"You forget that he dropped in at *Dido's banquet* this morning. I think he recollects enough of the old poem to know what comes next. And he must have noticed, Lucy, how you have run away from my assistance every night this week," her companion added, in a serious tone.

Lucy blushed as she said, "I thought you were not quite pleased with me; indeed I didn't know but this last week ―――― "

Morton took advantage of her hesitation to say, "You might deprive me of a very great pleasure—that of assisting you with your Latin lessons as long as I remain. Then I had something besides I wished to say to you."

"About the *poem ?*" Lucy asked, frankly.

"Yes! What made you think of that?"

"Because you never *have* spoken to me about it; and I am sure you don't like it."

"I *do* like it, every sentiment and every line of it; and yet its success gave me more pain than I should like to acknowledge. Shall I tell you why, Lucy?"

"I am sure I should like to know."

"I suppose you don't know anything about my plans for the future. I have never said much about them, for fear I might change my mind. When I set out to be a Christian, I resolved to do all the good I could in the world, whatever I might be called to do. I thought first I would be a teacher; then a minister; and afterwards I resolved to be both together, and go and carry the good news of the gospel to the heathen. Sometimes when I thought about it, it seemed like a great solitary work; but since I knew you, Lucy," he said, in a lower voice, "I have often thought, when I got through my studies, I would ask you to go with me, and help teach poor, ignorant souls of the Saviour who died for them. I heard uncle say once, you would make a first-rate missionary, Lucy.   But when I heard of the success of your poem, and knew that the paths of literature and **fame were** opening before you, and how well you would love to **walk** in those paths, I could not help feeling **there** was a death-blow to the hopes I had all along been cherishing.   **Do** you understand me?"

"I think so.   You were not displeased with me then, Morton?"   And a bright flash of light overspread her grave, serious face.

" I was never displeased with you in all my life," he answered in a low tone.   "I was only very sorry and disappointed.   I could not think you would be willing to forsake a life-path so pleasant, to go with me to a strange, benighted land."

"I have thought a good deal about being a teacher, if I could get prepared," Lucy replied; "but I never thought of leaving my home and country for ever.   Oh! how can *you* go, Morton?"

"How can I *stay*, rather, when I hear the Lord of the Harvest calling for laborers? Sometimes I think I should like to remain at home, and become a great man, and do something to be remembered by my countrymen in future years; and then the thought of *Him who was rich, and for* our *sakes became poor,* who was the Prince of Glory, and yet laid aside his kingdom and his crown for a cradle in a manger and a death on the cross, makes me willing to forget all my earthly ambition, and follow in his footsteps. I have a good many struggles, however, for I am naturally very proud and fond of distinction."

"Oh, so am I!" said Lucy, bowing her head as though the confession were very painful. "I never thought how proud and vain before." For some minutes she sat with her head leaning on her hand in silent thought, then said: "It has been a snare to me, Morton. Dear Mrs. Robbins often told me I ought to cultivate the talent given me for writing like any other of God's gifts, for the sake of exerting an influence and trying to do good in the world. But I am sure I have thought a great deal more about making a name, and winning praise and admiration, than of doing good."

"With the consciousness of being capable of surpassing others, it is very difficult to moderate one's ambition to the simple field of usefulness and duty. I know something about it by experience. When uncle says to me, as he often does, you know—'I expect to see you President of the United States yet, and make you a visit at the " White House,"' it rouses all the old desire for superiority, and I am almost tempted to cast off the mightier obligations of the Christian soldier, and enter a field where men and mind contend for precedence. Which would be the better way, Lucy?"

"You are not one who would abide by another's decisions, Morton; I learned that long ago. So if I were to tell you, you had better strive for the Presidency of the United States, or for some other office which calls for an equal amount of wisdom and judgment in the eyes of the world, I know you would not heed me. But whatever your own conscience says, I am sure you will do, whether it be hard or easy."

"God helping me to take up the cross of self-denial, *I will!*" he replied firmly. "And are you willing to listen and let conscience dictate your life-work too, Lucy? I don't mean directly, for one ought not to decide upon things of importance hastily. If I live I will come back here in a year, and you shall tell me your decision then."

Lucy made no reply; but there were bright shining drops trembling in her eyes, and ready to fall upon the open book, which as yet had the secret of the next day's lesson fast locked within its leaves.

CHAPTER XIX.

WHEN Doctor and Mrs. King returned, Morton and Lucy had translated the whole story of the Monster Horse which vanquished Troy, and were deep in Latin roots. No one dreamed what graver subject had lain in the foreground of the evening lesson. The doctor took the opportunity to lecture them on syntax, and showed plainly that the learning of his college days was not all forgotten. Examination-day was at hand, and he declared that any failure in the *Latin* class would be a mortification to himself personally, inasmuch as he had had abundant opportunities for drilling it and hadn't done it.

There was no failure, however, when the expected day came, for Morton and Lucy were not of those who fail in any undertaking.

To good natural qualifications, they brought unflinching purpose and untiring industry, without which no scholar ever yet made his mark. It has very truly been said, *there is no royal road to learning!* Along the same dry and dusty highways, and over the same rugged summits, the student of whatever name or rank must plod on and on, drinking at the same rills for refreshment. Those only who loiter and grow discouraged, find not the living springs which impart fresh strength to go for-ward.

Dr. King was delighted with the Latin exercises; so were some of the faculty of a neighboring college present on the occasion, who bestowed their commendations without measure. The compositions drew from them equal praise. One of these was declared to be so far superior to ordinary school efforts, that a copy of it was requested for the pages of the College Monthly. Lucy, whose composition it was, would have withheld it; but her friends overruling her determination, she was soon before the public again, more conspicuously than at first, her present article being prefaced by some remarks from one of the Professors, calculated to attract general attention to it.

It did not bring to Lucy's heart, however, a repetition of its former joy. Seldom has a second draught of praise the full sweetness of the first, under equal circumstances; and now new thoughts of life, and labor, and duty, were possessing her mind, and banishing the glittering dreams which for a while had charmed her young imagination, and made her unmindful of the sacred injunction, " Whatsoever ye do, do all to the glory of God." It still gratified her that her efforts should have won the commendation of her superiors; but there was no longer the feverish thirsting for approval, which imperceptibly even to herself had been checking her highest moral progress, and hindering her growth in grace.

Morton and Lucy parted without another word relative to the future. He had much study and preparation yet to make, before he would be ready to enter upon the work of his choice. Would he be able, amid all the temptations to which he would be exposed, to keep down the worldly aspiration, and remain true to his simple conviction of Christian duty? This was a question Lucy often asked herself as she went about her own homely duties during the long summer vacation. She had no doubt of it; for she fully believed that Morton King's fidelity to an honest persuasion, together with his natural steadiness of purpose, would prevail over any or every tempter which might assail him. The result proved her judgment correct. To ambition, wealth, and fame, leagued foes of the young Christian, he was able to say, "Get thee behind me! I have enlisted under another Captain, in another Cause."

There are more such heroes, my young friend, than the world has ever enrolled on her fame-list; but they are not forgotten by the King of kings himself, who will count all their struggles and victories in his service, and crown them at last *more than Conquerors.*

To no one, not even to her nearest friends, did Lucy speak of the new direction her thoughts had taken, since that single conversation with Morton King. His last words to her on the subject, "One ought not to decide upon things of great importance *hastily,*" were well remembered, and often pondered in her hours of self-communing and retirement. Was she willing to forego all her own plans for the future, to forget the sweet dreams in which youthful hope had loved to revel, to lay her home, her friends, and her beloved country —all these, with a second offering of self, on the altar of her dear Redeemer? It was a trying question, one not likely to be decided too hastily. It was a question to be wept over and prayed over in the silent hours, when the careless and the light-hearted sleep; when the Keeper of Israel, whose watchful eye never slumbers, bends low to his waiting earthly children. Lucy was often pouring the tale of her secret care into his ear, during those solemn watches when the world was wrapped in silence, until at last from the depths of her full heart she could exclaim, " Accept the offering, O Lord, though unworthy ! "

Morton wrote frequently to his uncle, and sometimes a note reached Lucy through this medium. He never questioned her decision, however, or referred to it in any way directly, though he often spoke of his own increased joy in view of his chosen work.

It was a season of great tumult and political agitation throughout the country, and while most of his fellow students were becoming violent partisans, Morton was able to look with an eye of steady faith to him who will overturn and overturn, until He whose right it is shall reign. How pleasant to think that while the earth seems shaken to its foundation by man's contentions, there are some who stand serene and peaceful upon this high mount of prophecy.

Never before had Morton experienced entire satisfaction in his choice. Hitherto there had been a mighty struggle in his mind between the way which conscience had marked out as the way of duty, and another path leading to heights giddy and bewildering. But now from his exalted stand-point, with the din of struggling factions in his ears, he could exclaim in fulness of heart, " He hath led me by a way I knew not of, and his banner over me is love."

36

CHAPTER XX.

WITH the spring that succeeded, fell another shower of divine blessing on the languishing churches of New England. From a few humble closets and lonely hearts had ceaseless prayers arisen, that the Lord would revive his work. The Lord has respect unto the lowly; His ear bendeth to their cry. Only a few feeble indications at first foretold the gathering mercy. Christians whose lips had grown unfamiliar with the language of Zion, and whose feet had strayed far away into world-paths, uttered low, broken tones of confession to their more faithful brethren.

Where a spark of grace lingers in the human heart, a little love-labor will soon prepare it for the full breath of the spirit of the Lord. Hence the blessed results so often attendant on Christian conferences and communings. From the hearts and homes of a few spread the warmth and glow which was felt that season in nearly every section of our beloved country. Colleges and institutions of learning shared abundantly in the work of grace, and none to a greater extent according to its size than the little pastoral seminary among the hills of Vermont. For some time had its members been the subjects of special prayer; and when the first seriousness became apparent, the pious teachers were prepared for the responsibility of their work.

What melting seasons of prayer and thanksgiving followed, as one and another of the beloved pupils expressed a wish to taste of the Lord's goodness, and to live to his service, can only be understood by those who have enjoyed a similar revival. How the hearts of old professors warmed towards the youthful converts just starting on the course they had been trying to run, and had run so feebly, as they confessed to them and to one another! and how earnestly were these exhorted in the outset, to leave behind everything which might prove a hindrance to their Christian progress.

Outside the school, no person seemed so entirely interested and absorbed in the revival as Doctor King, whose whole heart was enlisted in the work. No one had ever seen him so simply demonstrative before, not even in the former revival of which he was a subject. There was a lingering of reserve then, felt even by his most intimate friends; now, through his great, warm heart the love of Christ shone clear and triumphant. He was the first to point the trembling soul to the Lamb of God; the first to clasp the hand of the timid believer, and bid him have courage and be strong. With the double charge of church and school, the hands and heart of the faithful pastor seemed more than full; and a letter from Doctor King to his nephew at this time brought the latter very unexpectedly to Mr. Robbins's aid, with his heart all glowing with zeal for the cause of his Master.

Very affectionate were the greetings which . welcomed Morton back to his friends and fellow-students, many of whom recalled with grateful emotions his former kind admonitions and gentle Christian example. And now for the first time he made known to them his long-cherished plan of becoming a minister of the Gospel and a missionary to the heathen. It was at one of their meetings for conference, when Christians were moved to speak freely of the operations of the spirit within their own hearts.

Many listened to the confession of the young student with surprise; for, notwithstanding their convictions of his deep and fervent piety, they had long ago awarded to his superior abilities a place of lofty eminence and distinction among men. They had never thought of his forsaking *all things* for the Kingdom of God's sake and the Gospel.

His uncle was one of these; and when the long meditated design of his nephew was made known to him, he grasped his hand and with tears flowing down his cheeks, said, "It is better than the 'White House,' to go the Lord's ambassador to a heathen land! God bless you, my dear boy."

There was not a dry eye in the room as the doctor spoke, and every heart re-echoed his blessing. It is a touching sight when the young, at the call of country, forgetful of privation and danger, go forth to battle in its service. It is a sight to move the hearts of men and angels, when such are willing to take their lives in their hands, and go to the outer posts of self-denial and danger, in their Heavenly Master's cause. God bless the Missionary of the Cross!

The revival went steadily forward until not only the school-pupils but most of the youth of the town were numbered among its subjects. With these were both Harry and Charley Lee, and Lucy's heart overflowed with joy and thanksgiving for her brothers. A most affectionate relation had always existed between them, and except one point, entire confidence. Lucy had long understood Harry's desire for an education, and had encouraged him in every way to persevere in his efforts to obtain one. " Nothing is impos-, sible," she would say to him. " You can get thoroughly fitted for college here, fitted even to enter forward a year perhaps; then you can teach awhile, and I can help you a little by that time, I hope. All father will be able to do is to give you your time, but we can do your sewing at home, and you will be sure to get along somehow, for ' where there's a *will*, there is *always* a *way*.' "

But now Charley, who had hitherto been indifferent upon the subject, wished for an education too, and what could be done? Mr. Lee was not only unable to furnish the means, but could ill afford to spare both boys from the farm. He had always hoped one of them would be content to stay with him on the old place, he said, poor as the inducements were; but if it wouldn't satisfy them, they must go, and he would try to do the best he could alone. Lucy conversed frequently with her parents and brothers on the subject, and it was decided to be no more than right that the boys thenceforward should divide their labor, and have an equal.chance for an education.

CHAPTER XXI.

SOME time after Morton went back again to college, and things were going on in their customary manner in school, Dr. King invited Lucy to go and ride with him one afternoon, over the mountain. It was Saturday and half holiday, so she was much pleased with the proposition.

It was a long time since she had enjoyed her favorite ride. Doctor King took the same old route they had often pursued the summer succeeding her long illness, and it gave them a view of some of the finest scenery of the valley of the Connecticut. Lucy's love for the mountains had in no way diminished with years; and as they rode forward, or paused now and then to mark some feature of uncommon beauty or interest, her heart was too full for words. The doctor seemed in a less talkative mood than usual, and so for a time the ride promised to be a very silent one.

But when the last summit was passed, and they began the descent to the village beyond, where the doctor's errand lay, he managed to break the silence by saying, "I had a dozen things to say to you to-day, Lu, but couldn't possibly draw you out of the clouds when we were on the mountain top."

"But we are leaving mountain and clouds both behind us now," Lucy replied pleasantly.

The doctor seemed at a loss how to begin the conversation to which her frank reply invited; but after a little hesitation said— "Would you tell an old man a secret, Lu, after he had guessed it correctly?"

"I would tell *you* anything you should ask me confidentially, Doctor King!"

"Bravo! my child," he exclaimed, "for you and Morton *are* my children—all the children I have, and I have often puzzled my grey head to think how I could do something

for you both. I questioned him a little, but
he stands in need of no pecuniary aid, nor is
he likely ever to do so. Now what I wish to
know in the first place is, whether my sus-
picions are true, and you are to share his future
life-lot? "

Lucy's reply was an indirect one. " We
both wished to tell you," she said, with blush-
ing cheeks, " and——— "

" And so kept it still as mice from your
dear old uncle, who isn't quite blind yet, however, and who will give you a blessing with all
his heart. I always hoped you and Morty
would fancy one another, but never dreamed
of his making such a life-choice as he has done.
It is the best one, however, though it will be
hard for me to part with both my pets at once.
Another thing troubles me. You know my
income has always been all I could spend up
here, while my patients were sending beef and
pork, and corn and potatoes, enough for two
families to eat. Now, Mr. Robbins says he
will no longer take the hundred dollars I have

been in the habit of advancing him yearly, as the income from his school more than meets his wants. Why should I put it to interest when I have neither child nor chick to come after me? I tell you, Lu, I've thought a good deal about an old epitaph I've seen somewhere :

> " *What I spent, I had ;*
> *What I gave, I have,*
> *What I left, I lost!*

" Now I don't want *to leave* much to *lose*. I spend all I need ; but it is very little I've got laid up for the future world. It is too late for me to think of doing much work in the Lord's vineyard myself, but if I could help fit a laborer or two, it might be an acceptable eleventh hour service. I've been thinking about Harry and Charley, Lucy. They are good, brave boys both, and would, I am sure, with a little help at the outset, soon be able to make bold thrusts at error. They need an education for any profession they may choose, and since your father is not able to bestow it

unaided, why may not I be allowed the privilege of assisting?"

Lucy could not reply; she only took her
dear old friend's hand as he went on to say,
"You see I'm selfish in it all, child. I've
worked for self so long, it's hard to learn
lessons of pure benevolence now."

"You shall not talk so about yourself, Dr.
King!" Lucy exclaimed, with tears in her
eyes. "You are the most unselfish person I ever
knew, any way. From morning until night,
and from day to day, you are always doing
for somebody, or making somebody happy!"

"Hush, Lucy, and listen to me before you
eulogize me thus. Don't you see how my
locks are already as white as the blossoming
almond-tree, and how soon they must be laid
in the grave? Why should I not try to do
something which may be turned to my account
at last? Why, when my eyes are getting dim
to the world, and my strength fails, may I not
have the satisfaction of feeling that if I have
done but little myself, I have encouraged

others, whom I shall leave behind, to work for humanity and God?"

It was not often Dr. King spoke so earnestly, and as Lucy looked up and saw the warm, bright light that beamed on his open, honest face, she could not help saying, "What a great soul you have got, doctor! I can see it now shining like Jupiter among the little planets. I don't think any one need doubt that spirits *hereafter* will differ in glory, when we see them so very unlike *here!*"

"They *will* differ, my child—no mistake about it; but they will have to be weighed there in the great scale of *motive*, and I've no doubt that many a soul looked upon here as poor and niggard, will there outshine the brightest. Man sees no further than the outside, while to the eye of Omniscience all the thoughts and intents of the heart lie naked!"

A long and pleasant conversation followed respecting the influences which determine the human will, and direct its actions for good or evil, and upon the mysteries of those powers, moral and spiritual, whose operations are known only by their visible effects on the life and conversation.

Dr. King had thought much, and reasoned much. At one time, as we have seen, he was out on a wide sea of speculation, in depths too great for man's short line to fathom. Now, as he himself said, his bark had been wafted back by gentle breezes to the sheltering haven of his childhood. The same faith his mother taught him at her knee, was his polar star, by which he trusted, when his orders came, to steer steadily and safely into the port of Immortality.

CHAPTER XXII.

YEARS which have brought the young child to manhood, and laid old age to unbroken slumbers, have passed in swift succession since the commencement of our story. No town in all New England has been more blessed with health and happiness than our little mountain town; none more favored with spiritual and temporal prosperity. Everything now bears the marks of thrift and enterprise. The village is much increased in size, and numbers several very fine buildings, among which are a new and beautiful church, and a fine, spacious seminary. A few families of wealth and social position, attracted by the excellence of the school, as well as the healthfulness and beauty of the locality, have removed hither, and contributed to its general prosperity. A railroad has also been completed to a point not far distant, bringing with it some of the refining influences of the New England metropolis, as well as its luxuries. A ride of a few hours now transports the Bostonian from crowded dusty streets, to many a quiet summer retreat among the northern hills and mountains.

Among the new and benevolent features of our mountain town is a Missionary Society, which promises much usefulness. Its members are busily engaged now in preparing an outfit for one of their number. Morton King has completed his studies, been accepted by the Board, and is soon to sail for Asia. Lucy, a noble, talented woman, will accompany him. Never for a moment has she regretted the consecration of herself to such a work, though fraught with self-denial and sacrifice. Never do her young dreams of fame and worldly distinction cast a cloud over her future. Her pen is still the beloved companion of her meditative hours, and gushes of song, sweet as the

38

skylark's, often tremble and soar upwards towards the fountain of all inspiration.

She is home now, spending the last few weeks before leaving her native country, with her parents, brothers, and sisters. Harry is away at college, but is expected soon to pass with them his first vacation. Charley has been studying with Doctor King for nearly a year, and is already a great favorite with him; so great that the doctor insists, as soon as his lecture season is over, the young man shall take his saddle-bags, "step into his shoes," and leave him to enjoy slippers and rest as an old man should. Nothing could have been more gratifying to Lucy than this. That Charley should still be near her parents, with the prospect of being able to cheer and comfort them in their declining years, and be also the friend and helper of the dear old man to whom they all owed so much, was a source of greatest joy to her in the prospect of separation.

How everything had worked together for good

to them since they had loved God, was the frequent remark which fell from her lips. And the thought that, though widely sundered, they would all be at work in the same vineyard, in the service of the same good master, filled her at times with serenest joy.

> God's field is wide, God's work is great,
> And we all must help who can;
> 'Tis better than fame, to write one's name
> On the heart of a fellow man!

Such were Lucy's feelings poetically expressed. To lay the most shining gifts on the altar of the world, appeared to her far less great, and far less noble, than to stand forth a witness for God's truth. "Give not your youth to vanity, nor set your hearts on fame," were her frequent exhortations to her talented young sister; "but speak and act like a being endowed with a heavenly inspiration. Genius may be a dangerous gift. If you feel the fluttering of its wings, ask how you may best consecrate its powers to the service of God and Humanity. There are as many fields as gifts or laborers. Ask then in humility, 'Where will my Lord have me work?' and let simple, honest conviction decide the question. Mine is to be a distant field, but it is no further from our Heavenly Father's house than these beloved mountains. We cannot go to that house together. One by one, as we came to our earthly home, shall we go hence when the short work-day of life is over; whether from Asia or America, will matter little, if all safe together at last."

The thought of parting for life with Lucy, was a heart-breaking one to Ruth and Hetty, her beautiful young sisters. "To whom shall we go with our many hard questions and difficult problems, when she is gone?" was their oft repeated inquiry. "Who will tell us such beautiful stories of the stars and flowers, and show us how angels keep watch over the earth continually? No one can tell as sweet stories as Lucy."

"Ask rather how *I* am to live without her

who for so many years has been my best counsellor?" replied their mother in a softened tone, while she turned away to hide the tears she could not restrain.

But the time was drawing very near. Already the religious newspapers had announced there would be an ordination of missionaries in Boston on the first of September, and it was now August. Harry had got home, and Morton was expected in a few days. Twice a week the Missionary Society met now at the house of Mr. Robbins, and his wife had her hands full, cutting and planning, and packing away little parcels, to be opened by her young friend on a foreign shore. But everything was done in good time, and the last box stood ready for removal.

"She must be married in church," said one and another of her friends; "the whole parish will wish to witness the ceremony, and Mr. Lee's cottage cannot accommodate so many. Besides, Lucy belongs to the parish now, which has pledged itself to support her."

It mattered little to Morton or Lucy where the ceremony was performed, so they left it to be decided by their friends, who were unanimous in favor of the church. The young girls of the school, who had been Lucy's pupils, carried garlands, and put bouquets of the sweetest mountain flowers around the altar. Mrs. Robbins wrote a parting hymn for them to sing, and the whole congregation were weeping when the beloved pastor bestowed the final benediction.

The morning sun of summer was shining brightly without, leaving a glory upon the mountains, when the carriages and wagons laden with trunks and boxes paused before the church door.

If you have ever witnessed the departure of one under similar circumstances, you will understand what heart-wringing words of adieu are mingled with the tears and blessings showered upon the missionary bride, as she turns away for ever from the home and friends of her childhood.

A few carriages accompanied them to the depot, which was only a few miles distant, but by far the greater portion of the assembly were left standing around the steps of the church, waving hands and handkerchiefs until they were out of sight. Mr. and Mrs. Lee had parted with their child at home; they could not bestow their last blessing in the presence of strangers; so, as soon as the ceremony was performed, they turned away to their own home again, not even waiting to see the carriages depart.

The children all went to the depot, Harry, Charley, Ruth, and Hetty; so there was another leavetaking of the brothers and sisters, tender, solemn as eternity. They, who from childhood had shared each other's joys and sorrows, who knew all the dear home names and sweet home places, the trees where the robins built, and where the honey-birds hung their nests, the south hill-sides on which the first spring flowers blossomed, the meadows where the largest strawberries ripened, and the spring of the sweetest waters, who knew these, and all other dear places, such as every country household band have known and loved together, were to meet an unbroken band on earth no more. How many thoughts of the past and future rush into the mind in a single moment of farewell!

CHAPTER XXIII.

MR. and Mrs. Robbins, from the first, had agreed to accompany Morton and Lucy to Boston, witness the ordination, and see them on the ship which was to bear them afar. This was a great comfort to Lucy, for it seemed the last link was not yet broken which bound her to her native hills.

Next to her own family she had dreaded most the trial of parting from Dr. King and his wife, who had been second parents to her. It was a great relief and surprise to her then, when they arrived at the depot, to discover the doctor lifting a huge travelling portmanteau into the cars, and see him arrange seats for himself and wife directly opposite those which Morton had selected for themselves. "How very kind in you, dear Doctor King," was all

Lucy could say, as she pressed his hand to her lips.

"Not a bit of it," he replied, hastily brushing away a tear which threatened to betray his emotion. "I'm all out of medicine—have to go to the city once in a while anyhow; and there's wife who put her foot down she would accompany me this time whether or no. So you see nothing could be done but let her have her way for once."

Morton was no less affected than Lucy, by this last token of his uncle's regard. "I wished this more than anything else," he said, "but knowing how infirm you are, and how much you have overtasked yourself of late, I did not like to make the proposition."

"That is always the way with you and Lucy. One would never guess at your wishes if they didn't watch you pretty sharply. Then to think of my *over-doing* myself with that great boy Charley always on hand to help! He can already beat me springing a lancet or pulling a tooth, for his nerves are young and steady. Another thing which I wanted to go to the city for, was to see when the next course of Harvard Lectures begins. I mean he shall go to these right off, and be the sooner through. He don't mistrust a thing about it though, and you needn't tell him, wife, for I may change my mind."

The doctor's presence cheered them all the long way. His fund of stories and anecdotes was exhaustless, and he appeared to think the little party had need of some enlivening influence, so he exerted himself as he had seldom been known to do before, and the ride from morning until evening seemed neither long nor tiresome.

The sun was sinking low, when the grey shaft of Bunker Hill was discerned in the distance, and soon after the beautiful "City of the Bay" greeted their vision. At nightfall the travellers were comfortably established at the hospitable "Marlboro."

The next morning, after a drive around the city, they paid a visit to the vessel which was to convey the missionaries to a distant land. It was a noble ship, staunch and stately, looking as though it might bid defiance to storm and tempest. It was an object of admiration to Lucy, who had never seen an ocean vessel before, and who looked forward to the voyage with a pleasant interest. " Were it not for these bitter partings," she said, when their choice of state-room had been made, " I should be more than happy ! "

A few friends met them at the hotel that evening, and another young missionary pair, destined for the same field. " Henceforward we are to be *sisters*," the stranger bride said, as she kissed Lucy's cheek, while tears filled the eyes of each at the recollections which that word awakened. Heroic souls ! who, at the call of duty, go forth to combat error. Heavenly palms, instead of earthly laurels, await you. In God's name ye will conquer.

There was a solemn, quiet gathering the next day at the old South Church to witness the ordination of the missionaries. Few were present except the immediate friends of the parties; for although notice of the event had been made public through the religious papers, it was a time of too great national and political excitement for the people to heed the departure of a little handful of Christian recruits going to fill a broken company on a foreign shore.

At the same hour, a vast concourse thronged the open spaces around Faneuil Hall; banners were waving in the breeze; martial music was stirring the pulses of the crowd : eloquent lips were discoursing of patriotism, and pledging eternal fidelity to the Union and the Government of their fathers. A volunteer regiment was passing through the city on its way to the " Army of the Potomac," and citizens and soldiers were alike cheering it on its glorious errand. The carriages of the little missionary party, on their way to the place of embarkation, met the honored regiment, and Morton King, with a tear in his eye, lifted his hat and said fervently " God save my Country, and bless her noble defenders!" For a moment, perhaps, his thoughts reverted to his early dreams of fame and distinction; but no selfish regret was in his mind. The old thirst for superiority had long since subsided, and left only the purest patriotism and devotion in his heart.

"*All things for Christ!*" he exclaimed, as he met his uncle's eye fastened upon him as if to read the nature of his emotions at sight of the volunteers. "'*His* kingdom is an everlasting kingdom, and of his dominion there shall be no end.' Second only to His is the call of one's Country."

"You are right, my children," said the old man, with a quivering lip. "Fame, Ambition, Home, and Country even—ALL THINGS FOR CHRIST."